Ian Cochrane was
Irish author, his se
was runner-up for
lives in London and

Also by Ian Cochrane

GONE IN THE HEAD

IAN COCHRANE

F for Ferg

Futura

A Futura Book

First published in Great Britain in 1980 by
Victor Gollancz Ltd
This edition published in 1985 by
Futura Publications, a Division of
Macdonald & Co (Publishers) Ltd
London & Sydney

ISBN 0 7088 2702 0

ACKNOWLEDGEMENTS

Stuck on you, by Aaron Schroeder and J. Leslie McFarland, copyright © 1957 by Gladys Music, controlled by Chappell & Co Inc. Carlin Music Corp. for United Kingdom and British Commonwealth (excluding Canada and Australia).

Teddy Bear by Kal Mann and Bernie Lowe, copyright © 1960 by Gladys Music, controlled by Chappell & Co Inc. Carlin Music Corp. for United Kingdom and British Commonwealth (excluding Canada and Australia).

Reproduced, printed and bound in Great Britain by
Hazell Watson & Viney Limited,
Member of the BPCC Group,
Aylesbury, Bucks

Futura Publications
A Division of
Macdonald & Co (Publishers) Ltd
Maxwell House
74 Worship Street
London EC2A 2EN
A BPCC plc Company

F FOR FERG

FERGUS MOORE WAS new in the village. Well, he had been there for three months but nobody had got to know him. He came from the city. His Da had got one of the big houses just outside the village because he got the job as manager in the textile factory. We didn't like him. Partly because he was richer than all of us and partly because he had a better education. Anyway no one ever likes the manager's son. But Fergus wanted to be liked. He would ride past on his good bicycle and smile at us. When you looked at him, you could almost hear him saying "Like me." But all we ever did was throw things at him when he was going past on his bicycle. Sometimes one of us would tell him to get off and fight. But he never did. He just kept smiling.

One morning I was in the post office and he came in after me to buy a paper. I knew he knew I was one of the boys that threw things at him. But I said nothing. Then old Mrs Reed came out of the kitchen and she didn't know who to serve first. She was a fat little woman with a son and a daughter that looked about the same age as herself. She never wanted to do the job in the first place. I never knew why and nobody ever knew why she had no husband. They didn't talk as much about her because she was respectable in a way. You know, she tried to raise money for a playing field in the village and liked Scouts and all that sort of stuff. She did raise money for the playing field thing but it never got going right. Some of the committee said you had to pay to get into it and some people said it should be free. Then they said that there was to be no rough hooligans in it and they put up children's swings and the big boys broke them. Then some were barred and the ones that weren't barred got together with the others. In the end it turned into a kind of dump.

She came out of her living room and asked Fergus Moore if he was first and he said no, he thought it was me. I wasn't fussy, but Ma had always wanted me to get on with people with money. She never told me that, but I had felt it ever since I was born. As far as I was concerned people with money had manners, but one time I worked in a hardware shop and I found out that it was the people with money that never paid. So I'm not sure how I think.

"You go first," I say. "I'm in no hurry." Then I went and bought a stamp because Ma was going to send a letter to Uncle John in Canada. She had been meaning to write to him ever since he went away. He had been away over twenty years and kept sending us photographs of his wife and son. They always seemed to be standing up against a big car with sun hats on. Ma meant to send him a wedding present too. She bought a thing, but none of us could understand how it worked. According to what it said on the box, you didn't have to do anything with it. It should have sliced fruit and vegetables. The box showed you a woman holding up a plate of nice sliced fruit and stuff, and there was a well-dressed clean-shaven, white-toothed man standing behind her. And he was saying, HOW DID YOU DO IT SO QUICKLY DARLING? and she smiled and held up the contraption. Then he said on the box, WE'LL BE ABLE TO GO OUT TONIGHT DARLING. But it never worked and there was no need to send it.

When Fergus came out of the post office he had two or three magazines with him. I was sitting on the window beside the post box trying to figure out if Ma did send a letter how it would ever get there. I had no faith in postmen. The one we had would come to our door and talk for ages about fox-hunting, and the only thing he ever brought us was a big cake from Uncle John in Canada every Christmas. It was a great big heavy cake with a big hole through the middle of it. I reckon he was out of his mind because one time he wrote and asked Ma to send him some Irish grass. We never did anything about that, although Ma agreed with grass. She said grass and trees were lovely.

Fergus stuck a couple of stamps on an envelope and pushed it into the letter box.

"Have you got an uncle in Canada?" I ask him.

"No," he says. "I am writing off for a book that I don't seem to be able to get over here."

"Books are good," I say. Fergus had almost ginger hair, and a thin face and a black blazer with a cricket bat or something on it.

"What way are you going home?" he asks me. He smiled all the time.

"Well, I live up that way and I was to take this stamp home for Ma to write a letter to Uncle John in Canada."

"What part of Canada is he in?" Fergus asks me.

"I'm not too sure," I say. "But I could get the address for you if you want it."

"No, it's all right," Fergus says. "It's just that I was there for a while."

"Did you get your hair cut there?" I ask him.

"I did," he says. "Several times. I was there for over a year."

"Well, my uncle's a barber over there," I say.

"There's something very real about country people," Fergus says. "They think without knowing it."

"You must read a lot and everything," I say.

"It's not what goes into the mind. It's what's there in the first place," he says.

"Sometimes I wanted to join the library and get all them books."

"The mind tends to get rusty if you don't use it," Fergus says. "But maybe it is better living life." He sat down on the post office window beside me.

"You know," he says, "there is something natural about you. You don't have to think. You use your instincts. You're real."

"Have you got a girl?" I ask him. Then his nose starts to sweat and his face gets red.

"Oh, I don't bother about those silly little things," he says.

"We go up through the plantation every Sunday night and chase the girls," I say. "There's some good fun – Mary's the one."

"Is Mary nice?" he says.

"She's the one they all try to get but nobody gets anywhere," I say. "They all say they did, but I reckon none of them did." Fergus rolled up the magazines and pushed them into the saddle-bag.

"What's them about? Ma gets a woman's book every Thursday." It was true she did get one. It was full of pictures of nice clean women with nice clean aprons on too. But she never read it. She just started getting it one time a woman she looked up to told her it had good handy hints about housekeeping, and she never liked to cancel the order. The woman that told her to get it was a neighbour of ours when we moved into the council house. Ma liked her then, but her husband died and another man came to visit her before he was cool in his grave and Ma never spoke to her since.

"Just some magazines on hi-fi," Fergus says.

"They must be interesting," I say. I didn't know what hi-fi meant but I said nothing to him about it.

Then Fergus and me started walking down the street without thinking. I didn't want anybody to see me with him, but in a way I did. The boys all said he was a virgin and that he sat down to pee. But Ma was all on for him. She would be pleased. I would be bettering myself.

"What's this girl Mary like?" he asks me.

"She's a prick teaser. That's what they say," I say.

"You should think about higher things," he says. I didn't know what he meant.

"You mean motor cars and things like that," I say. He looks at me and I realize for the first time how ugly he is. His teeth are turning brown in parts and his skin is spotty and his eyes aren't even a real colour. His face doesn't look right either. It's like it is an old man's.

We walk down as far as Pot Stick Street and then we stop. I want to get away from him, not just because he's ugly but because he knows nothing about the village. I know everything and I know everybody. The Poet – what would he say if he saw me with Fergus? He would say something like, "Innocent white virgins in the black of night. Sucking warm milk from a cow." Or something like that, and Fergus would understand nothing. He might not know how to take him. But I know how to take the Poet. You just listen and say nothing. Then there was the men in Jack Robinson's yard. They would sit and look at Fergus and make remarks about Fergus being a Norwegian fruit merchant. That's what they called boys who liked other boys. And Fergus wouldn't understand what they meant. They all sat there all day and played cards in an old railway carriage. There was Jack Robinson. He owned the yard. He lost his eye in a factory in the town and made a fortune out of it and never worked since. The first thing he did was go to the bank and get a cheque book. Then he got rid of his wife. He set her up in a little bungalow and they never seen each other since. He bought everything he set eye on. He bought a baby's pram and he bought a lawn-mower – although he had no lawn. He bought a machine too for picking up leaves from a lawn and he bought a railway carriage and that's where Sam Kerr set up house. Him and Jack were in the same boat. Jack lost his eye and then Sam went and lost a couple of fingers and made a fortune too. In the end they closed that factory down because half the people working there had lost part of their bodies and had claimed compensation or hadn't come back after they had got the money, and the other half were on sick leave. You got so many days on the sick if the doctor signed a form for you, and he always did. But Fergus wouldn't understand that.

He wouldn't understand that because his father was the manager in the textile factory and he was there to make changes and folk wouldn't stand for it. That was partly why they didn't like him. Jack Robinson and Sam Kerr were Communists. They would stand for nothing from the big man. "We'll teach them – we'll drain the buggers dry," they would say. "We'll fight together. Together we shall fight, together we shall fall." And when Jack Robinson seen somebody going past in a big car he would spit and you could tell what he was thinking. Although when he first got the money, he bought a big car. He bought a big thing about a thousand years old and it used about a gallon of fuel a mile. It had big brass lamps on it and spoked wheels. Jack said it was an investment, but he didn't invest for very long because he spent nearly all his money and had to sell it. He sold it to a capitalist. That's what he said. He said to Sam Kerr that the man he sold it to could buy him twice over. Fergus would understand nothing. I wanted to tell him everything. I wanted him to be like me then I would have to tell him nothing. He looked at me with them eyes that hadn't even got a real colour and I felt sorry for him – him riding up and down the village all day just hoping to know somebody and nobody liking him. Poor Fergus.

"I don't think I'll go any further," I say. Then he looks at me and them eyes were crying. "Maybe I'll go a bit further," I say. We carried on walking down the street. Every now and then Fergus looked at me and it was as if he couldn't make me out or maybe inside he was crying. "We got a poet in this village," I say.

"Oh," Fergus says. "A real one? I have always wanted to meet a real poet. Poetry gives me such a pleasure. I like all poetry. All poetry that is written from the heart, I mean."

"Well, I don't think this bloke writes much. He more or less just says what comes into his head."

"You mean it's spontaneous," says Fergus.

"Well, I'm not too sure," I say. "All I know is that he has always been called the Poet. And he stands at the Methodist corner. That's why they call it Poets' Corner. He has never worked in his life and he says he doesn't intend to. Some folk say he's a lazy bugger."

"Poets shouldn't have to work," Fergus says. "They are God's gift to nature. The state should support him."

"All I know is that some people say he has verbal diarrhoea and they say he's a lazy bugger too. They say he is fit to work. He's fit to draw the dole and they say he never put a stamp on in his life. That's not what I say. That's what some folk say."

"What do you think of the old poets?" Fergus asks me.

"They're all much the same to me," I say.

"I'm very fond of the old poets," Fergus says. "They had something." If only people heard him talking! The folk in the village didn't like that kind of talk. Anybody who talked like that was a sissie. It was OK the Poet going over all that chat because they said he was mad too, and anyway he got fined once for asking a little girl to take her knickers off. If only Fergus would talk about dirty books or say what he did to girls then he would be OK. But he was stupid. He just talked all that highfalutin talk.

"Did you ever go with a girl in Canada?" I asked him.

"I would rather not talk about that," he says. And his face went really red again and his nose starts sweating. Then he starts coughing and couldn't stop. I should have thumped him one on the back but for some reason I didn't want to touch him. After a while he stopped and said he was sorry. It was odd. The only thing I ever heard anybody say after coughing was "Oh fuck, I thought I was going to choke." Or something like that.

"Would you like to be my friend?" Fergus says.

I couldn't – I couldn't. People wouldn't allow it. They would say things about me too.

"I've got a lot of friends," I say. Then Fergus stopped and looked at me.

"I have no one," he says.

"You're OK, your Da's got plenty of money." Then I looked at Fergus and I could see his eyes starting to melt, and his mouth started to go all kinds of odd shapes and he was crying.

"I have no one," he sobbed. "I just want a friend. Somebody I can talk to." Then without thinking I put my arm around him and I didn't care what folk said about me.

"I'll stick by you," I say. He still carried on crying and I squeezed him. "I'll stick by you," I say.

"I'm so lonely," he cries, and my spine felt a bit shivery. I wanted to take him into my arms and I wanted to carry him up and down the village and I wanted to shout, "Like him. He can't help it if his Da's got money." He brought out a really clean handkerchief and blew his nose.

"Thanks," he says to me. "Now I think I better be going home. Sorry if I have made a fool out of myself."

"You didn't make no fool," I say. "I'll stick by you. I'll take you to meet the Poet too. Do you know, I believe he is a real poet."

"Can we make some arrangement now?" he says.

"I'll meet you any time," I say. "I'm free all the time."

"Well, shall we meet tonight at the post office?"

"Right," I say. "I'll be there." He dabbed at his eyes with his handkerchief and I didn't want to look at him anymore.

"Right," I say. "I'll be at the post office." Then I left him.

The stamp had already got really dirty with all the things that had gathered in my pocket. Ma would say that she couldn't send a letter with a stamp like that. She would go on and on about it. She went on and on about everything, but she might be pleased that I had met Fergus. She might think that his Da might give my Da a better job in the factory. Da had one of the worst jobs going. Every night he came home and he smelt of bleach too. Ma kept on at him to get a better job, but he never did anything about it. Ma even bought him a paper that had all sorts of jobs in it, but he said he never had the schooling. He said he missed his chance at school. Da was always in the same job, but on his marriage certificate it said 'Factory Assistant' – Ma made him put that. She said it would look better in history if ever anybody was going to look back on it after Da and her were gone.

Ma went on about everything, but the thing that got her most was my brother Bill. He had to go into hospital for treatment because he was a schizophrenic. That's what the doctor said he had. The doctor told Ma and Da not to worry about it. It was just the same as a physical disease. He said that some great people had it, some of the wisest men in the world. But still Ma was ashamed. She told all the neighbours about it in the first place because the doctor told her that in some countries they treated schizophrenics as special people, but then she realized that that was in primitive tribes in some black place somewhere. The neighbour she fell out with told her that. She was an odd woman too. She bought books and things and listened to odd music.

Ma went on and on to Bill. If he wanted to go out she would tell him to stay in and if he wanted to stay in she would tell him to go out. Sometimes he would just sit there and stare out the window, not seeming to notice folk going down past. He would just sit there and stare. He would stare until his eyes would go all wet. I felt sorry for him when he was like that, but sometimes he would be different. Sometimes he would start talking and laughing, and he would say all the things he wanted to do. He would talk about all the good jobs he was going to go and get but then suddenly he would start crying for some reason or other. Fergus might understand him. Fergus is sad but he's deep. He might understand things like that. But Ma wouldn't want Fergus to know about Bill, not even when Bill has one of his good moods, because sometimes when he has his good moods he's odd too. He laughs and points at people and says dirty things. But Bill learnt a lot from the doctors. He knew what was wrong with him, and he knew all about all sorts of mental things. He told Ma she was suppressed and he told Da that he was suffering from an inferiority complex. Da tried to argue with him but Ma just give him a slap on the mouth. That was when Bill turned on her. He said that part of his trouble was due to her. That it was all her fault and if he could kill Ma then he would be cured. Then he sat down and talked out loud about how he would kill Ma, and she was sitting there listening to him. He said he might strangle her with a piece of wire or he might just slit her throat.

Ma told him not to be silly or he would have to go into the hospital and get more electric treatment. But it was as if he didn't hear her. "I might take a knife and just cut you up into little pieces. I might eat you." Then he looked like he had decided. "No," he said. "I want to strangle you. That will cure me." And he got up and made for Ma, and Da and me had to hold him back. Ma told the doctor and the doctor just shook his head.

The first thing Ma was upset about when I got home was the stamp. It was too dirty to send to Uncle John.

"Don't be bloody silly," Bill says. "It's the letter he wants to get, not the stamp. Or maybe he's a stamp collector. Maybe you just don't want to write. Maybe you're just wanting an excuse. Maybe you hate that silly bugger. Maybe you and him never get on. Maybe that's why he went away. Tell me. Now tell me, why did he go to Canada?" You could tell the way Ma's arm was twitching she wanted to slap him one across the mouth. But she didn't.

"He wanted to better his self," Ma says. "He wanted to make money. That's more than I can say for you." Then Bill's eyes started to stare and he starts as if he is just talking to himself.

"Oho. He wanted to better himself. Ha ha. Money, money. That's what's behind it all. That's what you want me for. You want me to make money. I suppose you want a fur coat or something. That's it. You want a bloody fur coat. Well, you married the wrong man. You married a useless man, a helpless man with an inferiority complex – an eejit of a man. I seen more sane men inside."

"Bill," I say. "Things are going to be different for you and me. We'll go out places."

He carried on talking – but not to me.

"Ah, we'll go out, will we? Maybe we better go out and work and get Ma a fur coat. Maybe the bitch should write to her brother for the money instead of pestering us." I went over to him and put my arm round his shoulder. Ma never did that because I think sometimes she thinks he might hit her or something. Bill's head was big. He had thick fair hair and a thick neck. When I looked at the big head I felt sorry for him. He was two years older than me. He was eighteen, but you wouldn't think it the way he acted sometimes.

"You're OK Bill," I say. He didn't look round at me, but he didn't try to shake my arm away either.

"Sick," he says. "That's what they say I am. Well, they'll not get me to take that electric again. They're trying to destroy me. Trying to get me to forget. I can remember nothing now." He shook his head as if he was trying to shake something out of it. "It's numb you see. I never wanted it in the first place. But that bitch . . ." Ma was looking at him as if he was sour or something.

"He can't help blaming you, Ma," I say. Then she started off.

"What in God's name did I do to deserve this. What did I do for this punishment. Maybe I have had my share. What do you have children for – to make you suffer. What will I do. God save me this day. I never had luck since I moved into this house. God take pity on me. God save me from this suffering."

Then she was crying and Bill was crying too. I pulled my hand away from Bill's shoulder. I didn't know what to do. I wanted to tell Ma about Fergus but she wouldn't listen now and Bill would sit and stare for a long time after he had finished crying.

I sat for ages and ages. Every now and then one of them would let out a loud sniff and I would know they were still crying. Da came in and nobody spoke. He didn't speak either.

He was used to coming in and the house like that. He went into the kitchen and started cooking something. Whatever it was he ate it in there too, and after he had finished eating he just sat in there for a long time. I reckon he had had enough. I reckon he didn't know what to do or say. After a while he came out and switched on the TV. He didn't look at nobody. There was a Western on. Bullets whistled all over the place. Da sat and stared at it, trying not to look at nobody. I reckon it was too much. Then after a while we were all looking at the Western and everything was all right again. In the middle of it I told them about me talking to Fergus Moore. Ma thought it was great. She said maybe his Da could get Da promotion in the factory.

"Like hell," Da says. "He sacked three men today."

"If they had been doing their work they wouldn't have got the sack," Ma says.

"They only went to the bog for a smoke," Da says.

"Well, that's wasting time," Ma says. "You can't pay men for smoking."

"If I get a chance, Da, I'll tell Fergus you work in the factory," I say.

"It would be a waste of bloody time," Da says. Then he just starts watching the TV again.

"Your Da has no push," Ma says. Then Bill bursts out laughing. His eyes are closed and he is laughing so hard you can't hear him. For a minute I thought that might be bad for him. He might just get hysterical like that and never come out of it.

"Push, push. That's what you need sonny," he says to Da, then he starts laughing again.

"It's not all that funny," Ma says. And that made Bill worse than ever. He was hysterical. He was pointing at Ma and saying, "Funny, funny." Then we were all laughing. We were all sitting there pointing at each other and killing ourselves. Then Ma said she had peed herself and that made us all worse. We all pointed at her, and then in the middle of it all Bill let out a fart and we got worse still. We were hysterical and I thought we would never get over it. Then suddenly there was a crack from the TV and the screen went blank and we all stopped laughing. Then we started again because it was so funny, us all sitting watching a blank screen. But Da didn't laugh any more. He didn't like the TV going like that. He went and moved something at the back and it came on again for a second. Then Bill stood up.

"Leave it alone. I'll fix it." And he did. He went over and did something at the back and the picture came back on again. He was great at doing things like that. We had a radio that didn't work and he took it to pieces and put it together again and it did work. After he did that sort of thing Ma always said he should be an electrician. Then Bill would say, "Nonsense, woman. I'm too smart to do anything like that."

"You've got a good brain," Ma says.

"I know," Bill says. "I know." As if he was just taking it for granted, as if nobody had noticed it before. Then he looks at me. "Well, I'll come with you to see this little pansy tonight," he says.

"All right," I say. "You come." Ma was in a good mood so she didn't try to get him to stay in. But she made him and me put on a tie before we went to meet him and she told Bill nicely to be nice to Fergus. She said that he could make a good friend.

"This is my brother Bill. He's a schizophrenic," I say to Fergus. Fergus gave Bill a warm handshake.

"How interesting," he says. "James Joyce was a schizophrenic."

"Never heard of him," Bill says.

"What do you want to do?" I say.

"I'm easy," Fergus says. "You do what you want to do and I'll tag along."

"We could go and chase women," Bill says. But he was only saying that to see what Fergus would do.

"I think that would be a waste of precious time," Fergus says. "Shall we go for a walk and a talk?"

"Balls," Bill says. "That's what I call a waste of time."

"Perhaps you're right," Fergus says. "You just do what you want to do and I'll tag along."

"We'll go down the village anyway," I say.

"It's a beautiful village," Fergus says.

"It stinks," Bill says and he takes a big hard sniff and spits.

"Well, you know it better than me," Fergus says.

We walked down the village. When we were passing Pot Stick Street, a group of boys whistled at us. Well, really they were whistling at Fergus. He still had on the black blazer, but underneath he had got a red waistcoat with brass buttons on it. I was waiting for Bill to say something about it. He kept looking at it.

"You look like a bloody Norwegian fruit merchant in that blazer," he says. Fergus blushed and said nothing.

"I think it's nice," I say.

"Balls," Bill says.

"I'm interested in the mind of the neurotic," says Fergus.

"How bloody stupid can you get?" Bill says.

Then Fergus blushed again and I felt sorry for him because he meant no harm.

"He's interested in things, Bill," I say.

"Who's to say who's neurotic and who's not?" Bill says.

"You're right," Fergus says. "Some of our great men were supposed to be neurotic."

"Are you neurotic then?" Bill asks Fergus.

"I am to some extent," Fergus says. "We all are to some extent. Nobody living in a repressed society can help it."

"You're not as neurotic as me," Bill says. "I have got all sorts of things wrong with my mind."

"Maybe," Fergus says.

"There's no maybe about it," Bill says. "I'm as mad as you can get. The doctor told me that I had to face up to it, that I was the maddest person that he ever met. He said there was no real treatment for it either. He said that I was an interesting case and one day he brought about a hundred students to see me. They asked me questions and agreed that I was really mad."

"That's interesting," Fergus says.

"It's bloody interesting," Bill says. "I was in the loony bin for six months and they never got me put right. Do you know, I painted pictures in there to see if I could find out more about my mind. The doctor said that the pictures told him nothing. But he showed them to the students."

"How intriguing," Fergus says.

"Did you know I hit a nurse across the mouth for nothing," Bill says.

"There must have been a hidden motive," Fergus says.

"Well, you could say that," Bill says. "I wasn't too keen on her. She had a big mouth. But after I was in the hospital a while and got used to her, I hit her every day she was on duty. I just slapped her across the mouth. One day I was in the bathroom she came in and asked me to hit her. I never hit her after that and she left before I did."

"Did she remind you of anybody?" Fergus asks.

"No," Bill says. "I just didn't like her big mouth."

"It's odd," I say.

"Why don't you get a job in the factory if your Da's the manager?" Bill says.

"Oh, I'm waiting to go to Oxford," Fergus says. "English and French."

"Is there any money in it?" Bill asks.

"No," Fergus says. "But they are very interesting subjects."

"You'll need to read a lot of books," I say.

We were coming up to Poets' Corner and the Poet was there. He was standing there with his hands on his hips as if he was taking a sermon or something. His hair was long and he wore a coat with wide sleeves. He looked a bit like the bloke I saw in a book at school one time. A bloke that could talk to the animals and all the birds came and sat on his arms.

"This is Fergus," I say to the Poet. The Poet folds his arms and looks at Fergus. Fergus put out his hand to shake hands but the Poet just eyed him up and down. Then he says, "Fergus. From the Latin *fergue* to fuck."

Fergus didn't know what to say and he looked like he didn't know what to do with his hands either. He looked like he was always trying to hide them. Bill starts laughing.

"What do you think of the waistcoat, Poet?" he says.

"Yes, I have been looking at it," the Poet says. "The blood-red blending into the golden buttons. The fragrant smell of a boy in his youth. A young maiden warm on the chest. Beauty is in the air – in the sweet breath of nature. It is a lovely waistcoat. A rich red." Fergus was well pleased.

"Thanks," he says. "What do you think of Keats?"

"Marvellous chap," the Poet says. "A man. A real man with deep brown arms and the mind of a woman in the evening air."

"There's not many people around tonight," I say, because there was usually a few people gathered around the Poet.

"They are in the warmth of their homes. Dreaming of beauty. Sucking the air into their hearts . . . snug beside their fires . . . warm in their mother's breast."

"I thought there might have been more people out tonight than there is," I say. The Poet looked at me as much as to say the subject was closed. He had said all he was going to about the matter. He was still looking at Fergus. He started at his feet and went up then he started at the head and went down. Fergus still didn't know what to do with his hands.

"You are restless young man," the Poet says. "Do I smell a sweet smell of spring? Do I hear little virgins rising?"

"I've read a lot of poetry at school," Fergus says.

"Young man, I have read more books than you'll ever see. I have ploughed through some of the greatest works ever to be written. I have travelled. I have seen skies the colour of rainbows and clouds as soft as a flower."

Then Fergus didn't know what to say.

"He wants to be mad like me," Bill says.

"The brain is sweet when it is covered with petals, covered with wiseness, drowned in the fountain of knowledge."

"Balls," Bill says.

"That's interesting," Fergus says. "Do you think knowledge is everything?"

"Everything and nothing. It holds the beauty of darkness in its heart. It soaks in the wisdom of old men. It reaches out and touches the little dewdrop."

"You must know everything about nature," Fergus says.

The Poet lifted his hands up in the air. "I am Nature," he says. "I am in Nature and Nature is in me. The birds sing in my brain, the lion rests in my heart."

"Jesus Christ," Bill says.

The Poet paid no attention to him. He kept his hands up and swung himself around. Then he plucked a leaf of the laurel bush that was growing up behind the wall. He reached it to Fergus.

"Take this from me, son. Press it in your heart tonight.

Dream on the clouds. Let your dreams wander into a maiden's heart."

Fergus took the leaf and looked at it.

"It's a marvellous thing," he says. "Do you see the design in this? I'll keep it and press it into a book. I've got a whole book of pressed flowers." Then he slipped it into his pocket.

"I'll tell you you should be locked up," Bill says. The Poet looks up the street.

"Here comes the man with the charm. The man who can bring little maidens into his heart."

It was Rab that was coming. He had long hair too. He grew it when he was in England. He had bright blue jeans that he got in England too. His jacket had big padded shoulders and he got it in England too. He walked with a slight swagger of the shoulders. You would think he owned the village the way he walked down the street.

"Big head," Bill shouts at him. He didn't speak till he came up to us.

Then he says to us, "This is a bloody dead village. Look at it." And we looked up the street.

"This is Rab," I say to Fergus. "He was in England two or three years ago." Fergus stuck out his hand.

"I lived in London for two years," he says.

"Son, you have never lived," Rab says. "Have you been in Soho? Have you seen the ladies on the Bayswater Road?"

"No," Fergus says. "I never got time for that." Rab looks away as much as to say it was useless talking to Fergus any more.

"I love travel," Fergus says.

"Let the sweet mind roam," the Poet says. "Let it drift into the summer air."

Rab paid no attention to the Poet either.

"You want to see some of the pros I got when I was over

there. I went with this one one night. God, she was good-looking. She had breasts like melons. God, they were big." He waved his hands over his chest to demonstrate to Fergus how big they were. Fergus made a surprised sound then he blushed. Rab went on, "We went to bed and stayed there for two days. Do you know, she wanted to marry me. She said I was the best man she had ever had. My God, did she go! But I gave it to her. 'You're great,' she said. 'You're the best man I have ever been with.' And do you know she told me she had been with over a hundred men. She cried when I told her to get out of bed. And after that I had a letter from her every day. She used to write with lipstick. But I couldn't see her because I was going out with this little blonde thing from the East End. She was a very possessive little thing. When girls smiled at me in the street she used to get very jealous. In the end I had to tell her to go. She wanted me and her to go away. She said she would get some money together for both of us. But I wouldn't go. I liked her OK but she was too possessive. She would never let me go out with another girl. Do you know, one girl's not enough for me? I need about three."

Fergus was standing there listening with his mouth open. Bill was sniggering because we always heard these stories about him in London. He would change them round a bit each time.

"It's a lot of balls," Bill says.

He always said that after Rab had gone on for a while. Then Rab would say "I can prove it," and Bill would say "Prove it."

"I can prove it," Rab says.

"Prove it," Bill says.

Then Rab brought out his photographs. He handed one round of a big blonde girl. She was wearing a bra and knickers.

"That's the first girl I went out with in London. The one I was telling you about that wanted to marry me. That's her before we went to bed." When Rab handed the photo to Fergus, Fergus blushed like anything and the sweat was pouring out of him too. "Never be shy with women," Rab says. "I never was. I just used to go up to a girl when I was in London and ask her would she sleep with me. What the hell, what have you got to lose? They can only say no. Mind you none of them ever turned me down. Do you know what size my prick is?" Fergus was sweating more than ever.

"No," he says, and went into a fit of coughing.

"Do you want to see it?" Rab says to Fergus.

Fergus stammered for a while then he says, "I wouldn't mind."

"I'm telling you it's big," Rab says to Fergus.

"Is it true you can balance six pennies on it end to end?" Bill says.

"Sweet the smell of the body. The odour of love hangs on the pubic hairs," the Poet says.

Rab opened his flies and brought out his prick. It was reasonably long with a kind of purple head. You could see the sweat dripping off Fergus. The steam was rising off him.

"I think the mind should be put to higher things," he says. Rab stood with it hanging out and his hands in his pockets.

"Take a good look at it," he says to Fergus. "You'll never see one like that again. About ten girls in London told me it was the biggest that they had ever seen, and they had been around a bit. You know I don't believe in virgins. I hate them. I like girls to have a bit of experience."

Fergus kind of looked at me and it was as if he was crying out for help. It was as if he was trying not to look at it.

"Take a good look," Rab says. "Tell me what you think of it. Tell me, did you ever see one like that before? Did you?"

"No, I haven't," Fergus says.

"This is where all the big nobs hang out," Bill says.

"I bet you you never seen one like that before," Rab says to Bill.

"Put it away," Bill says. "You should be ashamed. I would bring mine out only I don't want to shame yours."

"Come on," Rab says, "hang it out. Come on. I bet you a fiver that mine is twice your size."

"Where's your fiver?" Bill says. Rab brought out his wallet and handed the fiver to me.

"Here, you hold the money," he says.

"I don't want to show you up," Bill says.

Rab took the fiver back as if he had just won a bet. "I know mine's the biggest," he says. "This thing could win competitions."

He told Fergus to have one last look at it and then he put it away. After that he asked Fergus two or three times if he wanted to see it again. Fergus blushed every time. Rab went on and on about the women he had been with in London. Then a few little girls came down the street and Bill asked him to prove himself. Rab said he didn't want to get jailed for baby-snatching. The little girls were all dressed up in little pink coats and straw hats. They were always around the village. They were only about ten but they still went out looking for men. You always seen them up the plantation on a Sunday night.

When they walked past I said to them, "Will you take me with you?" They all giggled and blushed. Then after they were past a few yards they stopped and one of them shouted, "Jane loves you, Johnny." Then the one that was called Jane hit the other one and shouted, "I do not." I closed my fist.

"Guess what I have in my hand. Guess what I have got and you can have it." One of them tried to push Jane down towards me. I had nothing in my hand. I just wanted her to come down to me.

"Get stuffed," Bill shouts.

"You go and get your head seen to," one of them shouts.

"I'm wiser than you," Bill shouts. Rab paid no attention to them. It was as if they weren't there. And anyway he wanted to get peace to do some more talking.

"Maidens come and brush my hair," the Poet says. "You little virgins, warm from the womb, clean and white, as soft as a flower."

"Come and see what I've got in my hand," I shout. The one that was called Jane had nice black hair, and big black shiny eyes. Her eyes were full of mischief too. The Devil was looking out of them.

"It's interesting how poetry has changed through the ages," Fergus said to the Poet. The Poet said nothing. He was lying against the wall looking at the little girls.

I held out my closed fist. "Come on and see what I've got," I shout.

Jane came towards me a few steps then she started giggling and ran back to the other two. Then they started whispering and the three of them came towards us.

"Jane wants to know if you love her," one of them shouts.

"I've never said nothing," Jane shouts. They were only a few yards away and they stopped.

"I'll not touch you," I say.

"Come and give her a kiss," one of them shouts, and Jane goes to run away and they stop her. I make to run towards them and they all scream. But they didn't move very far away.

"I'll not touch you," I say. Then I run straight for them. They all tried to get away, but they were still running into each other. I caught Jane. She was giggling like anything. I held her tight and tried to kiss her, but she put her hand over her mouth. Then she took her hand away and I almost did it but she put her hand back again too soon for me. I got my arms round her waist and pulled her up to the church gate.

"Kiss her," the other two little girls were shouting. I held her tight with one arm and opened the church gate. She didn't pull back too much and I was able to get her right into the bicycle shed at the back of the church. We lay up against the wall and she tried to keep me from kissing her but not as much as before. After we were in there for a while, I was able to kiss her all the time and she didn't mind. But she wouldn't let me put my hand up her leg.

"Go on – let me. I'll do you no harm," I say, and she let me put my hand up a little bit.

"I don't want a baby yet," she says.

"You're OK," I whisper and I get my hand up a little bit further.

"Do you love me?" she says.

"Yes," I whisper and she let me put my hand right up to her knickers.

"You're only saying that," she says.

"No, I mean it," I say and we kissed a lot. Her lips were burning and between her legs was really warm too.

"Will you take me out for a walk some time?" she says.

"Maybe next Sunday," I say. Her hair smelt clean and it tickled my lips. Her lips sucked at my neck. She was nice and warm. It was nice feeling her soft clothes too, and her warm lips. I was tight up against her. She pressed tight against me too.

We stayed there for ages. It got nicer and nicer. I wished that nice tickly feeling could stay there for ever. Then it had gone, everything had gone and I felt wet and sticky between my legs. She must have sensed what had happened because she put her hand down and touched me and then she gave me a kiss as much as to say "You're a good boy."

When we came out there was two or three more people at the corner. There was Jack Robinson and Sam Kerr and the singer.

Jane ran up the road to where the other two little girls were sitting on the wall waiting for her. Roy, the singer was called. He liked me because I always told him what a great singer he was.

"Did you get it, Johnny?" he asks me.

"When I was that age I was with a little girl every night," Jack Robinson says.

"This is Fergus," I say to Roy. Then I look at Fergus and he is shaking. He can hardly speak.

"Are you all right?" I say.

"I feel a little bit weak, Johnny," he says. "It must be this fresh air."

"What does your old man do with a house that size?" Jack Robinson says to him. Fergus giggles a little bit and says nothing.

"I bet you he never worked for his money," Jack Robinson says. And he spat right at Fergus's feet. "Where did you get that waistcoat from?" Jack says and Sam Kerr gave a loud laugh to himself. Him and Jack never spoke to each other all that much. They just mainly tried to get each other's money.

"He can't help it if his Da's got money," I say.

"Dad," Jack Robinson says, "Dad, it's Dad in his circles." Then he spat again at Fergus's feet. Fergus looked as if he wanted to move away but he was too scared.

"Maybe your Dad would like to throw us a few crumbs," Jack says. Fergus kind of looks at me for help.

"He seen what I've got," Rab says. "Didn't you?"

"Yes indeed, I did," Fergus says. He wasn't shaking so much now.

"Tell them what you thought," Rab says.

"I thought it was enormous," Fergus says and he was pushing at the spit with his toe. Then he looked up and he didn't know who to look at and he looked back at his toe. Sam Kerr didn't talk as much as Jack Robinson.

"How many rooms are in that big house?" he says to Fergus. Fergus looked up again.

"Twenty," he says.

"Nobody needs a house that size," says Sam. "There's something wrong somewhere. The world's not right divided."

It was almost dark. You could hear the rumble of the factory further down the river. We were all silent for a while.

Then Jack Robinson spoke again. "I suppose you're a bit of a brown bomber," he says to Fergus. Then he looked at us. "That's what they do in these big posh schools. You see there's nothing but boys there."

"How about a song?" I say to Roy.

"Ah, I'm in bad voice tonight," he says.

"What do you sing?" Fergus asks him.

Roy didn't answer him. He just burst into song. It didn't take much to get him going. He was like Elvis Presley. He stuck his leg out and shook it like Elvis too.

Right in the kitchen, right in the hall
Ain't goin' to do you no good at all
For once I catch you and the kissing starts
A team of wild horses couldn't tear us apart.

He pretended to play the guitar too. After he finished we all clapped except the Poet. Fergus clapped too. The Poet just looked at him.

"The sweetness of the voice is like the breath of spring to the ear. The pleasant hum of the bee. The sweetness of the lark up in the blue. Singing to the world. Listen, listen. It sings for you. Yes, it was a good song."

"Shakespeare said, 'If music be the food of love, play on,'" Fergus says. Everybody looked at him as if he was mad.

"He reads a lot of books," I say. But still there was silence. "He can't help it if his Da's got money," I say.

Jack Robinson spat. "He's not giving much of it away," he says.

"No indeed," Sam Kerr says. "There's not much money going round at the present time." Jack Robinson looks at him.

"Why?" he says. Then Sam Kerr spat.

"There's money somewhere," he says.

"And do you know where it is?" Jack Robinson says.

"It's somewhere," Sam says.

"I think Marx had something," Fergus says. Then they all looked at him and then at one another.

"How much would your Dad be worth?" Jack Robinson says.

Fergus looked as if he was thinking for a while. Then he says, "The trouble is, if you gave everybody ten pounds at the beginning of the week, by the end of the week some would have more than others. It's just nature. We are all different."

"Who's filling your head with that crap?" Jack Robinson asks.

"What about another song?" I say to Roy. He started straight in:

Just a want to be, your loving teddy bear.
Put a chain around my neck and lead me anywhere.
Just a let me be, just a let me be,
Your teddy bear.

"I used to sing when I was in London," Rab says.

"Balls," Bill says.

"You go back to Moy Abbey," Rab says. Bill didn't like people saying that to him. That was the hospital he was in.

"You shut your face or I'll slap you one," he says.

"You and who else," Rab says.

"It doesn't matter whether you sang in London or not," I say. It was bad to get Bill too excited.

"I sang all over London," Rab says. "Everywhere I went people were asking me to sing. One night a crowd of girls thought I was Elvis Presley and they wanted my autograph. I could have got off with any of them. They were screaming. I took their addresses but I never had time to contact them. Mind you, there was a few pretty ones among them. I was tied up at the time with two little blondes. They were both mad on me. They both knew about each other, you know. But they didn't mind. I used to leave one and she would cry because I was going to meet the other. You know I'm a bit of a hard bastard as far as women are concerned. They can take it or leave it. I'm not worried. There's plenty more fish in the sea."

"Who the hell wants fish?" Jack Robinson says. And everybody laughed.

"Tomorrow's the day the cow calves," Sam Kerr says. That meant that it was the day we got the dole money. We were all on it. The man and woman came out every Friday to pay us. The thing is, if you lived a mile out of the town you had to go into the Labour Exchange three days a week and if you lived two miles out you had to sign on twice a week. Then if you lived three miles out you only had to sign on once. But we lived five miles out of the town and nobody could agree on it so in the end after we went on a kind of strike they decided to come out and pay us. You see there was no rule at the Labour Exchange to sort that out. We didn't really go on strike. We had to sign on a Friday. So what we did, we all got in there just five minutes before closing time and they had to start signing us on and paying us out and that meant they were there very late. We should have signed on at nine-thirty in the morning. Anyway it was something like that.

That's how I tried to explain it to Fergus. He walked up the street with us a bit although he lived down at the other end of the village. Then I tried to explain to him that Bill didn't have to sign on because he was on the sick. He got his money from the Ministry of Health or something, although he had a bit of trouble getting it at first. The doctor gave him a certificate and he sent it off a week later and then he got it back with a letter asking him why he hadn't sent it sooner. It said he was to give an explanation. The thing is Bill was in bed taking big tablets that made him sleep all the time and he couldn't send it. That was before he went into the hospital. So he wrote and said he was asleep and then they sent the certificate back with another letter that nobody could understand. Bill still had the letter and he showed it to Fergus. It said:

> If you have sent a certificate claiming for sickness benefit from the time you were sick then you are entitled to sickness benefit. If however you haven't made a claim during your recent illness and have since started work you may not be entitled to the benefit from the 20th. However if you want to claim you may send the certificate no later than three days after first becoming unable to work. You will receive the money within twelve days from the date on the certificate. You should state on a B2 why you were unable to send it. A B2 can be obtained from your local Ministry of Health. If someone claims on your behalf you should state why.
>
> No certificate should be sent to this office if the person is

employed or if he is abroad. You may send more than one certificate at once if you have been ill when you first received your first certificate from your local GP.

If the person does not qualify for sickness he should go to his or her local Social Security Office and obtain a G3. This should be sent to us immediately.

Fergus said it was the system. He said he could understand it to some extent but that it could be made a lot clearer.

But the main reason he came up the street with us was because he wanted to know what I did with little Jane behind the church. Well, he didn't ask me outright.

"I enjoyed this evening," he says.

"It was OK," I say.

"What part of the evening did you enjoy best?" he says in a matter-of-fact kind of voice.

"I'm not too sure," I say.

"It was a laugh, you and that little girl," he says. I laughed. "Do you think that kind of thing is good fun?"

"It's all right," I say.

"He's always doing that," Bill says. Fergus seemed surprised.

"It must take a bit of nerve," he says.

"You just go and do it," I say.

"I wish I had the nerve," Fergus says. "But your instincts are more primitive than mine."

"What are you on about?" Bill says.

"Did you laugh a lot when you were in there with her?" Fergus says.

"No, not much," I say.

"He was too busy looking for her pussy cat," Bill says. Fergus blushed and coughed.

"What did you do?" he says, as if he just didn't care. He just said it straight out.

"I felt her leg and kissed her," I say. Fergus wanted to know something else, but maybe he didn't know what or maybe he didn't know how to say it.

"Do you want to talk about it?" he says.

"Well, I'm not fussy," I say.

"Well," he says. "Did you enjoy it?" He was like one of those interviewers on the TV.

"I did," I say.

"Do you do it often?" he says.

"Well, now and then," I say.

"With the same girl?" he asks

"Not always," I say.

"Do you think it's right to flirt around with girls? I mean don't you think it's better just sticking with the one?"

"Well, it doesn't really matter much," I say. I felt he wasn't really asking me what he wanted to. He thought for a while. Then he says, "I don't think you should go too far."

"Well, you go as far as you can get," I say.

"I suppose that's pretty far sometimes." He gave a kind of giggle.

"I reckon you got cancer," Bill says to him. "You don't look all that healthy. You're very thin and everything." We walked in silence for a while. Then Fergus looks really serious. There was no trace of a smile on his face, and there was usually a trace of a smile even when he was blushing.

"Do you really think so?" he says.

"Well, I knew a chap when I was in hospital," Bill says. "He looked just like you. He was really thin and had bad skin like you. He died before six months were out. It can't be cured, you know." Fergus went really white and I seen his face in the street light. It looked like he might cry.

"There's people as thin as you live for years," I say.

"If I were you I shouldn't take no long term obligations on," Bill says.

"Shut up, Bill," I say.

"Maybe I better have an X-ray," Fergus says. "Will you come with me, Johnny?"

"I'm not sure that I believe in X-rays," I say. "There was nothing wrong with my Granda and they gave him an X-ray and he died after that."

"That's right," Bill says. "Sometimes they can kill you. Why don't you just go and jump over the bridge and it'll save a lot of bother."

"Maybe it wasn't the X-ray that killed my Granda," I say. "He was nearly ninety."

I didn't know whether Fergus was serious or not about the X-ray. But he was. Next morning when I went to sign on he was standing there with the appointment card. I think he felt better after the doctor gave him that card because he was smiling again. He had to go to the town on the Monday to have it done. He said he wasn't scared about it. He had one when he was at school and there was nothing to it. Then he starts explaining to me how an X-ray worked. He talked about rays and things. Then he started on something about light waves and things. I wanted to shut him up because he was standing in the dole queue with me and the people in the dole queue don't like learning. They don't like people that know a lot. Then he starts going on about the system. About how the dole works and the Government and things like that. And nobody wants to know things like that either.

Jack Robinson was at the front of the queue. He was always in the front. "How many rooms is it your dad has?" he shouts to Fergus.

"Twenty," Fergus shouts back and everybody starts clapping.

The man and woman sat down at the little table all ready to pay us out. As soon as they sat down we all clapped again. They weren't too pleased about that. They never wanted to pay us in the first place. Still it's not a very safe job because two or three times the little man got thumped by somebody and every Friday morning while we were queuing we planned how we could rob them, because after they left us they had to go and pay out in another village so they had plenty more money. We had plenty of plans but the main one was just to thump them one.

Jack Robinson got his money and he stuck it in his hip pocket and walked out. Everybody cheered and shouted, "What are you going to spend it on?" Then the next thing I knew he was back in again, and his face was red. There was a kind of hush and he walked straight to the little man. He said something to him and the little man shook his head and signed for the next person to come and get his money. He was doing that as if Jack wasn't there – as if he had no time to waste. Then Jack caught him by the chin and turned his head towards him. You see Jack claimed for his wife and for some reason or other they hadn't given him anything for her. Suddenly Jack lifted the table and sent the two officers flying. The money went flying too. There was no queue any more. It was a free-for-all. I forgot about Fergus and got in so that I would get my money too. I could smell nothing but men pressing against my nose. Somebody nipped me and I nipped somebody else. Then there was a lot of kicking and we all seemed to fall at the same time. Then there was a kind of groan and we were all up pushing and biting and pulling. I felt something – it was money. I held it tight and somebody was trying to press my hand open. But I held on to it and got away. When I got outside, Fergus was standing there as white as a sheet. I had got four and a half pounds. Normally I only got two. Everybody that came out looked happier than usual. Everybody had managed to get more money than usual.

Jack Robinson led the way and we all went up into Sam Kerr's railway carriage to play cards. Fergus wanted me to go for a walk with him, but I couldn't. They would think I was a sissy too. I wished he hadn't come with me because he kept asking me questions. First he wanted to know how old the carriage was. Then he wanted to know who made the stove. It was just a big barrel with a hole in it and a drainpipe going up through the roof for a chimney. Fergus thought it was great. But we all knew it was a terrible thing. It wasn't well made and it didn't burn. Then he didn't understand the cards. He didn't know what we meant when we said that Jacks were better or if we said I'll see you and raise you or I'll go blind. Then Jack Robinson asked him if he ever tried taking a long walk off a short pier. And he tried to work it out.

The men didn't say very much to Fergus. They mainly said things to each other. But really they were speaking to Fergus. They said things like "There's some people who can't stop talking," and "Some people have a big mouth." But Fergus didn't know they meant him. The thing is you can't play cards right with somebody talking to you all the time, asking daft questions. In the end when I had lost half my money we left. Fergus kept on about wanting to go for a walk and talk. But I didn't want to go. I didn't know what I wanted to do.

"You're real," he says to me.

"Well, everybody is more or less real," I say.

"What I mean is you're unspoiled," he says.

We sat on the wall at the corner and didn't know what to talk about.

"What would you like to talk about?" Fergus asks.

"Anything," I say.

"What interests you most?" he says. Then he looked up the street and you could almost see his eyes getting bigger. It was Mary coming. She was wearing a lime green dress and she had beautiful brown legs. Her dress was well above her knees too.

"That's Mary the prick teaser," I say. Fergus didn't speak. It was as if he had gone into a trance or something. Mary took nice little steps. She always walked with her head slightly down, as if she were shy. She always smiled and blushed too. She had lovely skin and eyes that darted from one thing to another. She went past a couple of yards then stopped.

"Johnny, I want to talk to you in private," she says. And I went up to her.

"How's it going?" I say. She kept her head down and examined her little fingers.

"Oh, all right," she says. "I suppose you haven't seen KZ," she says. She meant Stewart because he had a big car and the number-plate of it started with KZ. She was mad about him and if he stopped in the village in his big car she would get me to take messages to him. He was loaded with money too. He never worked for it either. His father died and left it all to him. He had thick curly hair and a big brown face. She thought he was the greatest. She loved him like anything, but he didn't love her. I saw him in the town two or three times with different girls, but I didn't tell her that because he had taken her for a drive a few times. He was a big hard chap. He had everything. His car was the biggest around our way. I don't think he was really serious about anything, because when I took messages down to him from Mary, he would give a big laugh and ask me if she wanted stuffed or something. I never told her that. I made up things to tell her. If I had just given him a message and he drove straight past her, I would tell her that he had to go somewhere to collect his mother. There was nothing went around in her head all the time but him.

"I think he doesn't like me," she says and then she put her head down in that pitiful way to make me say something nice to her.

"I think he does," I say.

"What makes you think that?" she says.

"I'm not going to tell you," I say. I had nothing to tell her. I just wanted time to think something up.

"Oh, come on, Johnny, what makes you say that?" she pleaded.

"Nothing," I say.

"You're a sly devil," she says. "You know something that you won't tell me."

"I'm saying no more," I say. She pulled out a packet of cigarettes that she had stuffed up her sleeve and gave me one. We stood there and lit up. She did that to make me talk.

"He was in the village one night and you weren't out and he asked me where you were," I say.

"What did he say?" she says.

"He says 'Where's Mary tonight?'" I say.

"Why didn't you come up for me?" she says.

"I thought you might be away somewhere," I say.

"How did he say it?" she asks. I made my voice sound really interesting and said it over again to her. Then she got me to say it two or three times to her.

"If you were him what would you say to me?" she says. I thought for a while then I said, "Mary, I like you a lot." She blushed slightly and gave a little giggle. Then I had to say that to her two or three times.

"Do you think he would go out with another girl?" she says.

"No, I don't think so," I say. Then she says as if she didn't care anymore,

"No, he's not interested in me. Why should he be? I'm

nothing to look at. I'm sure there is plenty of really good-looking girls he can get. What would he want with somebody like me?"

"He thinks you're really good-looking," I say.

"You're having me on again," she says and gives me a little push.

"No," I say. "He thinks you're great. He told me that he thought you were the best-looking girl he had ever seen. He said he thought you had great legs too."

She was really pleased.

"If you see him don't tell him about anything I said. It's just between me and you. Promise now." I promised. Then she whispered to me, "That fellow keeps looking at me." I looked round and there was Fergus staring at her. "You should know me the next time you see me," she says to him and he looks away.

"I think he likes you too," I say. She let out a loud laugh.

"Oh, God Almighty, I wouldn't be seen dead with him."

"He's OK," I say.

"He makes my stomach turn to look at him," she says. "Look at that face."

"Bill says he's got cancer," I say.

"It wouldn't surprise me," she says. "Now remember, what we were talking about is just between me and you."

I promised not to say anything and she went away. Fergus's eyes followed her up the road.

"Do you know her well?" he says to me.

"I talk to her a lot," I say.

"Is she interesting to talk to?" he says.

"Well, she's OK," I say.

"That's what one needs. An interesting girl," he says.

"Did you ever meet any interesting girls in Canada?" I say.

"Not really," he says. "It was a boys' boarding school that I was at there. Mind you it was very interesting, but you didn't get much of a chance to meet stimulating girls."

"That's odd," I say. We walked across the bridge and up the road.

In the morning the sky had been clear but now little clouds had gathered and got thicker and thicker, choking the sun. They seemed to be squeezing the earth. The birds had stopped singing. You could just hear the noise of our feet on the road.

"How do you get on with your Mum?" Fergus says, and he kind of startled me because for some reason I had been thinking that I was alone.

"OK," I say.

"Do you mind if I tell you something?" he says.

"No," I say. Then we walked on in silence for a bit before he told me.

"One night I couldn't get to sleep and my Mum came up and got into bed beside me. Dad was away at the time. Maybe I better not tell you."

"That's OK if you don't want me to know," I say.

"I might as well tell you," he says. "I know you can keep a secret. Well, Dad was away. The thing is she kissed me on the lips."

"Ma never kisses me," I say.

"I used to keep thinking about it," he says.

"How long ago was that?" I say.

"Three years ago," he says.

"Have you forgot about it now?" I say.

"Not quite," he says. Then he looks at me kind of quick. "Do you think I should tell Dad?"

"Well, you could if you wanted to," I say.

"No, but do you think I ought to?" he says.

"Maybe she has already said to him about it," I say.

"What makes you think that?" he says.

"Well, I just think she might," I say.

"Perhaps you're right," he says. "You think by instinct more than anything. I often think that that's the best way."

"Well, I'm not sure," I say.

Poor Fergus. He doesn't understand and maybe I don't understand him. We walk along the road and I can see his face all rough and pimply. Bill might be right. He might have cancer. He might die. I could see him in a coffin. Him just there and he never did understand nothing. The sky got heavier and heavier. Just our steps in the silence.

"I'm enjoying this walk," he says. "We must do this more often."

"The weather's got very close," I say.

"Has it?" he says. "You must be more sensitive than me about things like that."

"It's one of them days that's heavy," I say.

"Was there boys and girls at your school?" he asks me.

"Yes," I say. "I never heard of anything different around here."

"I think that's a good idea," he says. "It teaches you not to be shy with girls. Did you learn much about sex at your school?"

"No, just what I picked up," I say.

"Did you have lectures on it? You know the way they have in most schools now."

"I think you just know them things," I say.

He thought for a while. Then he says, "Perhaps you're right. After all it is an instinct. You don't get talks on how to eat – it comes naturally."

The sky was very grey now. It was very heavy on my head. We turned into a little lane. A bird gave one little chirp and fluttered in the hedge. The lane was hard and rough. Fergus didn't seem to be too good at walking on it. He seemed to stagger about, but he didn't say anything. We turned into a field. It was half ploughed. It had been half ploughed since ever I can remember. We sat down on the grassy bit. The grass was kind of soft and warm. Fergus sat close to me. I didn't like him to be too close in case he had germs or something. There was no noise at all. Fergus was silent too. We were alone in the world. This big silent world with just me and Fergus. I felt a bit scared. Then I took a deep breath and I felt a bit better, but it was hard to breathe. The air seemed thick. Far down across the little hedges over half-ploughed fields, over cornstacks that had been there for ages too, there were cows, black motionless cows. Not even eating any more. They might be dead too. The fields got blacker and blacker as they stretched into the sky. The sky was black down low too. If you went further through the blackness there might be the sun. It's odd, the thick grey air. Maybe if you fell you would go down and down for ever. I can't think that – it scares me. But I can't help thinking it. Down and down into the thick grey air. Then it gets blacker and blacker. No light, just big black mouths open. Then there is big orange balls and then a big black crack. I feel Fergus's hand on my leg. There is a flash and another big crack.

"Thunder," Fergus says. I get up. His hand falls away as if he didn't even know it was there.

"It's going to pour down," I say. I made towards the old hen house that was further down the field. That had been there ever since I can remember too and there was never a hen in it either. But when I got in I realized that there must have been hens in it some time or other because the floor was thick with hard dung. Fergus came in just after me, and I sat down on one of the perches. There was a little window with no glass in it. There was one hard crack of thunder and rain was pouring down. It was thick like grey glass rods. There was no world outside. Fergus put his hand into my arm.

"It's a little bit frightening," he says. I didn't speak and I didn't like to push his hand away. There was a bright flash and then a little rumble in the distance. It got louder and louder. Fergus pressed closer to me. The rumble got louder and louder and then ended with two or three loud cracks. The rain hissed down heavier than ever. Fergus was looking at me out of the side of his eyes for some reason.

"You're sensitive to the weather," he whispers.

I felt stiff. I felt as if I was in a kind of trance. Slowly the kind of weight started to lift from my head. I felt as if my skull was opening and my head was getting lighter. There was a light steady strone fizzling on the ground. Fergus was looking at me out of the corner of his eye. Then I saw his hand coming up and resting on my leg again. I said nothing. I pretended it wasn't there. Then he started to rub it up and down. I looked at him and he stopped.

"I hope you don't mind me doing that," he says. His face had gone kind of funny – as if he was thinking about something else.

"No," I say. I remembered when I was about nine or ten. This nice boy came to live near us. He had a lovely face and his eyes always seemed to twitch into a smile. We went up into this place among the trees and played with each other. It was great. We were very fond of each other. Then one day I looked up and his mother was watching us. She didn't allow him to play with me any more.

Fergus was rubbing up between my legs. I didn't love him but it was getting hard all the same. He was looking at me and he was really ugly. I felt a kind of anger come into my belly. It gave a little heave and my eyes got wet and I felt sorry for him. His face all pimples and kind of greasy, and there was little bits of grey saliva at the corners of his mouth. He was kind of staring and he was opening my flies at the same time. Then suddenly my stomach started to boil and I grabbed him round the throat. He put his arms round my neck and we fell on the hard dung. I could feel his skin warm and slippy. I was pulling at him and he was breathing hard. I could feel him opening my trousers but I didn't stop him. I squeezed at his neck – but not too hard. Then he had my thing in his hand and he was pulling at it. It was nice. I just held him tight and let him do it.

Then we both sat up. The rain had stopped and the sky was blue again. Dry hen-dung was sticking to my skin. I stood up and brushed it off and pulled up my trousers. None of us spoke. We got out and started walking. There was a strong smell of earth and grass. I was going to mention it to Fergus then I thought I better not bother. Out in the lane the rain-drops dripped from leaf to leaf then onto the lane. The birds had started to sing again and there was lots of other noises in the distance. A dog barked and another dog answered. A motor saw screamed its way through logs. The world had come to right again.

Fergus was the first to speak when we got down into the village. "I hope you are still friends with me," he says.

"I am," I say.

We stopped at the corner again. There was little rainbows on the wet road where a car had dropped oil. Fergus looked at his big watch. "Would you like to come to my house for tea?" he says.

"Your Mum or whatever you call her might not like that," I say.

"No, she won't mind," he says.

"All right, I'll come but I'll not stay too long."

We started walking towards his house. You could see the big thing on the chimney that told you what way the wind was blowing long before we got to the house. There was a lot of trees round it. There was big white pebbles in the drive. Fergus opened the door for me. The house smelt of polish and clean things. There was lots of shiny pots and pans hanging all round the kitchen. He opened another door and two big dogs jumped up on us. Big white dogs with black spots and big black droopy mouths. One of them licked me right on the mouth. Fergus told them to sit down and they both went into the corner and sat down on two big white velvet cushions.

"They know what you say," I say.

"Dad has them well trained," Fergus says.

The room was enormous. There was great big chairs and great big clocks and great big long lamps. Everything was old too.

"It's a nice place," I say.

"I quite like it," Fergus says. "But it's not as nice as the house we had in London."

"Was that nicer?" I say.

"Oh yes, much," Fergus says. "Mind you, it was more modern."

A woman in a green overall rushed in one door and out the other.

"That's not your Mum?" I say.

"No," Fergus says. "That's our daily, Mrs Blane." Then I remember who Mrs Blane was. She used to live in a house in the village long ago. The house belonged to the factory. Then her husband died and she left the house in the village and moved into the big house and she was never seen since. That was fifteen years ago and some people said she was dead.

"Some people say she's dead," I say.

"Who? Mrs Blane?" Fergus says. "No, she's as fit as you and I. We took her on with the house. You could say she is part of the furniture. She's a great help to Mum. We have given her a little room of her own up at the top."

"Well, you never see her out anywhere," I say.

"No, she doesn't really go out," Fergus says. "You see we have a Swiss girl who can drive the truck and she does most of the shopping. Mind you, Mum enjoys shopping herself."

"My Ma does all her own shopping too," I say. "Sometimes she gets me to do it, but I don't like to. I thought that other girl I seen around was your Mum's sister or something. She looks a bit like her."

There was just the sound of all sorts of clocks ticking. Fergus went into a corner and lifted a big wooden lid up.

"Would you like to hear a record?" he says.

"I wouldn't mind," I say.

"What would you like to hear?" he says.

"Have you got *Goodbye Johnny Dear*?" I say.

"No, I haven't," he says. "Do you like Mozart?"

"I'm not sure," I say. He set the record on. You could hear everything really plain, as if you were in a big hall or something. There was a big box on either side of the fireplace and that's where the sound was coming from. Fergus came over and stood between the two boxes and listened hard. Then he went back and turned a knob.

"That's better," he says.

"It sounds like a good record-player," I say.

"It's pretty good," he says. "We had it built for us. You see the acoustics are very good in this room." I looked round.

"Is that right?"

Fergus went and sat down in a big chair and closed his eyes. There was a lot of instruments playing all sorts of things and you could hear a little click every now and then. The two big dogs lay with their paws out and their mouths resting on them and their eyes closed too. There was a kind of thud upstairs, but I said nothing. I just closed my eyes too.

I heard a door open behind me and I opened my eyes. Fergus got up.

"Mum," he says, and they kissed each other on the cheek. "Mum," Fergus says, "this is my friend Johnny." His Mum didn't pay any attention to me.

"Darling, your jacket's damp," she says. "Go and change." Fergus went out. His Mum came over to me. She had brown skin and long thick black hair and she was wearing trousers too.

"You're Fergus's friend from the village," she says.

"Well, you could say that," I say.

"Fergus has been telling us about you," she says.

"He told me about you too," I say. She laughed.

"Oh dear, what has he been telling you?" she says. "Nothing bad, I hope."

"No, he never said nothing bad."

"Now, would you like some tea?" she says.

"Well, that's more or less what I come for," I say.

"I'll call Mrs Blane," she says, and she went out. Then she came back with a newspaper. "Would you like to put this over the back of your chair?" she says. "I think your hair might be a little oily." I felt a bit angry because nobody had ever made me do that before. But I put it over the seat all the same.

Mrs Blane came in and rushed into the kitchen. "She's an odd woman," I say. "Some people think she's dead." Fergus's mother looked a bit startled.

"Oh dear," she says and gave a little giggle.

"Nobody's seen her for fifteen years," I say.

"She's rather shy," she says.

Fergus came in with a coat on.

"Does that feel better, darling?" his Mum says.

"Yes Mum," he says.

"You will catch a chill again if you don't be more careful," she says.

"I never bother changing," I say. Fergus went and turned the music down a bit.

"It's a lovely record, darling," she says to Fergus.

The tea was ages coming. I heard the clatter of cups two or three times and I thought that that was it coming but it wasn't. I was starving. If I had been at home I could have just gone into the kitchen and got a big slice of bread and jam or maybe bread and butter and syrup. I wanted to go home. I was thinking about Bill. He wasn't too good when I left in the morning. He wasn't speaking. Ma reckoned she was going to have a bad day because she said he was in one of his moods. Ma asked him if he wanted an egg for breakfast and he didn't answer her. Then she boiled one for him anyway. He just cut the top off it and pushed it away. Then he emptied out the tea she had given him and filled the cup up with milk. Ma said nothing to him after that because she was scared in case he might fly off the handle.

The kitchen door opened in the big house and I thought the tea must be coming this time but it must have just opened on its own because Mrs Blane pushed it closed again. I looked at the clocks. They all more or less said half past four.

"What time do you usually eat at?" I say. Fergus looks at his watch.

"We usually have tea about this time." Then he says to his Mum, "It's taking Mrs Blane an awful long time." His Mum said nothing. She was busy looking at a magazine. Then the door opened and Mrs Blane pushed in a whole trolley-load of stuff. She didn't speak and she didn't look at anybody either. She had a red face. It looked like the blood was about to come out through her skin. She left the things and went out the other door.

There was little squares of bread not much bigger than a stamp. They had all sorts of things on top. The only thing I recognized was the ones with parsley on them. Fergus's Mum poured out the tea into little flowered cups. I went to put milk in mine and Fergus told me not to. He said you must never put milk in China tea. I thought that all tea was from China but I didn't say. It tasted a bit like some kind of soap, but I was glad to get it. It wasn't like the tea Ma made. You could never be sure how her tea was going to turn out. Sometimes it was almost white and half-full of sugar and sometimes it was almost black and half-full of sugar. And when it was cold and she re-heated it, it usually turned out a grey colour. Our cups weren't really cups either. They were big mugs. As far as I can remember Ma got them for drinking a lot of cocoa. She had to send all the labels away, and all that time we got no tea. We had cocoa with everything. When you put boiling water in them they made a kind of hissing noise.

"These are nice cups. Did you get them in the town?" I say. Then there was a sort of silence. "They don't look strong," I say. Still nobody spoke and Fergus's Mum looked at him as if he had said something wrong. I knew that it was something to do with me but I couldn't figure out what. Then I dropped a bit of something off my bread and one of the dogs came over and gobbled it up. This seemed to upset Fergus's Mum too. She said to Fergus that the dogs' food had been weighed out in the morning. Fergus said that he thought a little bit extra might not do them any harm.

I can tell you one thing, I was glad to get out of that house. It was good to see everybody standing at the corner. Fergus didn't come with me because his Mum said that he had to have a hot bath after getting wet.

"That was a laugh at the dole this morning," I said. But none of them spoke. Not even the Poet. "I was going to stay and play cards longer only he wanted to go," I say.

"Your little sissy friend," Jack Robinson says.

"He doesn't seem to know much about cards," I say.

"Them's the men that grow up to rule the country," Jack

says. They were all kind of silent. I wanted them to talk to me. I wanted things to be the same as they always were.

"I never made friends with him – he made friends with me," I say.

"Why don't you go home?" Sam Kerr says. Then he spat.

"The crumbs of the rich man's table are sweet," the Poet says. "The grass in his lawn is green. His heart is rich. The poor eat the grass."

"You didn't get a bit from his Mum," Rab says. "She's not a bad-looking thing. I have a good mind to go up there one day myself and show her what it's all about. I'm sure that old man of hers can't do much."

They all laughed.

"Did you lick her arse?" Jack Robinson says.

"I wanted a cup of tea and he asked me to go to his house. That's all," I say.

"Is your Ma's tea not good enough for you now?" Sam Kerr says. "You'll be getting a good job down in the factory."

"What about a song?" I say to Roy. He didn't speak, he just looked at me. They were all looking at me.

I went to lean against the wall like the rest of them but Jack Robinson pulled me away.

"You'll dirty your coat," he says, and he brushed it with his hand. But he didn't mean it.

"I tell you," I say. "I'll tell you," and I was nearly crying. "I went up there just because he asked me. I wanted to see what it was like. But I didn't like it. I was a bit scared. They had two big dogs and it was all odd. They put on funny music and his Ma made me put a newspaper on the back of my chair because I might put oil on it. And I seen that odd woman that everybody said was dead. She made tea and I took one sip and threw it on the floor. Then I says I'm a Communist – that's all."

They were all laughing.

"Is that true?" Jack Robinson asks.

They were all laughing like anything.

"It's true all right," I say. "I took one mouthful of tea then I spat it out and emptied the rest on the floor. 'Don't give me any of that bloody stuff,' I say, 'I want real tea.' And his Mum's face went red and I say, 'Come on, come on. You don't need a big house like this. You just start giving it to folk that need it, I say.'"

"God almighty, you're a smart boy," Sam Kerr says and he could hardly speak for laughing.

"When I was going out the door I told her to get stuffed," I say.

Then I heard Rab saying, "I'd stuff her – capitalist or no capitalist."

"I'm proud of you," Jack Robinson says. Then I started to feel a bit off. I started to feel sorry for Fergus for no reason.

"You know Fergus," I say. They all said they did. "Well, I feel sorry for him. He's got cancer."

Then I realized maybe I shouldn't have said it because they said that Jack Robinson's Ma died from cancer and every now and then he got drunk and cried about it. That's why he got rid of his wife. Because she wasn't as good to him as his Ma was. He said that nobody could take a mother's place.

"Oh dear," Sam Kerr says. "It's a terrible thing. Money can buy you a lot, but it can't buy you health." Everybody agreed and Jack Robinson said he knew all about it and nobody asked him any questions.

After that I wasn't too sure whether I wanted to see Fergus again or not. But I couldn't do anything about. He called up to our house. I didn't tell him the number we lived in. He must have asked somebody and everybody knew. Bill was in an odd mood and I thought he was only having us on. He was sitting at the window.

"There's your little pansy friend to see you," he says. Ma just started and she went round the house like a madwoman. She stuffed things under cushions, she stuffed things behind big calendars that we had got for buying coal. We had five of them – all different years and each one had a big tree on it. Then she was going to Hoover the mat before he came in but she couldn't because I had broken it. I was trying to invent a thing for peeling potatoes. There was a little hard brush went round in it and I reckoned that if you held a potato against it, it would take off the skin. But it didn't. It spun the potato out of my hand two or three times and then when I held it really tight it kind of screamed and stopped. But it would be OK. Bill would fix it.

Ma gathered up the potatoes and threw them out the back door then she hit me a couple of slaps and ran up the stairs. She didn't wait to see if it was really him.

"He's coming in here," Bill says. "Look at the way he walks."

"It's not him," I say.

"Well then, don't believe me," Bill says. Then the door got a knock.

"Tell him I'm not in," I say to Bill.

"I'm not telling lies for you," Bill says. And he went and opened the door.

"Come in, come in," he says to Fergus. Fergus came in and stood there. He looked a bit odd standing in our house after me seeing him in his big house.

"Sit down," Bill says. "You'll not find no comfort here. I hear you got plenty of nice furniture in your house. And I hear you got two big dogs too. What do you want them for?"

"They're Dad's," Fergus says.

"They're Dad's," Bill acts him. "What have you got that big thing up on top of your chimney for? Can't you tell what way the wind's blowing without that?" I wished I hadn't told Bill about being there. Ma came downstairs and she looked like something out of a comic or something. She had her hair all up in kind of grips and she had bright red lipstick on and her face was as white as snow with powder. She more or less looked like a snowman bleeding.

"What are you, a gypsy or what?" Bill says.

"This is my Ma," I say to Fergus.

"Very nice to meet you," Fergus says, and stood up and shook hands.

"Very nice to meet you too," Ma says. "My son has been telling me a lot about you. I hear you have got a nice house." Ma was talking like some of them people you get in the town.

"It is quite nice," Fergus says.

"They got two bow-wows too, Ma," Bill says. Ma looked at him and made a kind of face telling him to keep his mouth closed or she would close it for him. I don't think Fergus seen her.

"What are you making that face for?" Bill says. Ma laughs.

"My sons are full of fun," she says. Fergus laughs too.

"Mum says it would be a poor world if you couldn't laugh," he says.

"Did she say that?" Ma says. "She must be a happy woman."

"She has her moments," Fergus says.

"I hear you got two dogs," Ma says.

"Yes, we have two," Fergus says.

"I love dogs," Ma says. "I think they are the best friends you can have. You can't keep them in the estate."

"You can give them a good kicking and they'll come up and wag their tails," Bill says. "Do you know that, Fergus? Do you know anything about dogs? I studied them once, you know."

"I once read a book about dogs," Fergus says.

"Books," Bill says. "I read two or three hundred books about dogs. I could tell you anything you like about them. I know their minds better than my own."

"I'm very interested in animal psychology," Fergus says.

"I think you should never hit a dog," Ma says.

"Do you know anything about elephants?" Bill says. "I know everything about elephants there is to know. An elephant has tusks three feet long and a short tail. You get them in the jungle. They eat lions and all sorts of things. I read this book about a wild elephant and do you know, it could climb trees."

"Shut up Bill," I say.

"An elephant has a brain the size of a bucket of water," Bill says. "It can think better than a dozen men put together."

"I think cats are not so nice," Ma says.

"They are very independent creatures," Fergus says.

"Did you hear the one about this woman fed her husband on cat-food?" Bill says. "The shopkeeper said to her that she would kill him. She said that it wouldn't. Then one day she went into the shop and said her husband was dead. I told you, the shopkeeper says. It wasn't the cat-food that killed him the woman says. He was running along the wall and he turned round to lick his arse and fell off." Bill went into hysterics after he told that. Fergus kind of laughed. Ma's face was red as anything.

"My husband works in your father's factory," Ma says.

"Does he?" Fergus says.

"Yes," Ma says. "He loves it."

"Maybe we better go out for a walk," I say.

"Would you like a cup of tea?" Ma says to Fergus.

"I would love one," Fergus says. Ma rushes into the kitchen and you could hear everything flying. The next thing was she came out with the big mugs and a tray full of plates of little squares of bread with sauce on them. The tray was one Bill made in the hospital and it wasn't very well made.

Fergus said he wouldn't have anything to eat, he would just have the cup of tea. But Ma forced him like anything and in the end he ate one of the little squares of bread with tomato sauce on it.

Because it was Sunday night we had to dress up to go out. I had a green plastic tie. It was one of those ones with a piece of elastic and the knot was already on it. Bill had one too only his was blue. When we were getting ready Ma came up and told us how nice she thought Fergus was. She said he had lovely manners. She said why couldn't we be like that? Bill paid no attention to her. He got this razor blade and pretended to cut his throat.

Fergus shook hands with Ma before we left too. Ma was well pleased. She told him to come up and visit us any time he wanted.

"I like your Mum. She's a natural," Fergus says.

"Like hell," Bill says.

We went down through the village and up along the road that went through the plantation. There was lots of little girls walking up and down in little groups.

"You'll have to chase the girls," Bill says.

"They won't take to me. I'm a stranger around here," Fergus says.

"It doesn't matter," I say. "Sometimes boys come from other villages to get girls here."

We stopped about halfway up and sat on the wall. The first two girls that came along was two little blonde sisters. They were so blonde you would think they had just been through a flour mill. One of them had good tits and the other one had none at all. I grabbed the one that had got good ones and got her up against the wall. She screamed but I didn't let her go till I had kissed her. Bill kept shouting all the time.

"Get in there," he shouts. Then the sisters run away.

"You do that next time," Bill says to Fergus.

"Should I?" Fergus says.

"You do it," Bill says. "There's nothing to it."

The next to come along was three little dark-skinned girls. They were sisters too and their oldest sister had to get married because she was expecting a baby from some bloke from another village and he drank a lot. So they didn't get married in the Methodist church in our village and they didn't live there after they were married either. I waited till they went past then I went and grabbed one of them from behind. They all screamed. But I held tight. She was strong and pulled me along the road a bit. Then we both fell. The other two ran up the road and started shouting. I grabbed her tight and gave her a good kiss before I let her go. Then she came back and said that she wasn't scared of me and I got her again and gave her another kiss. Her two sisters were well up the road and she had to run to catch up with them. They shouted that they were going to tell their Ma.

Fergus couldn't make up his mind whether to do it or not. He was sweating but he wanted to do it.

"You catch the next girl that comes along," I say. "She'll not bite you." Fergus said he would give it a go.

The next two girls that come along were pretty big. They were about twenty.

"The bigger the better," Bill says. Fergus looks at me to see whether he should or not.

"What have you got to lose?" I say.

"Right," he says, and the sweat was almost dripping off him. They went past and I thought he wasn't going to do it.

Then Bill says "Go!" And he went after them. He was just

about to grab one when the other one seen him and swung round with her handbag and hit Fergus straight on the mouth. He went down. The girls walked straight on. Then when they were well away they shouted at Fergus:

"That's nothing to what you'll get the next time. You dirty bugger! Away home and grow up."

Fergus just sat there on the road with the blood pouring out of his lip. I went and helped him to get up.

"You get that sometimes," I say. He couldn't speak for a while. He had a big white handkerchief and he dabbed at the cut.

"I better go home," he says.

"Don't be a sissy," Bill says.

"I thought you did well," I say. "They hit you sometimes even if they like you."

"Is that right?" Fergus says.

"You just sit up on that wall and try again," Bill says.

When I saw little Jane coming along I told Fergus to wait there and I would be back. She stopped and her and me went up through the trees. From right up there you could see the whole village. We sat and looked at it. She said she wished she had left school and she wished she was away from home too. She asked me if I thought like that and I told her I did. We said we would marry each other and live in a little house. I was going to build the house and she was going to plant the garden full of flowers. Then she cried and told me that somebody had told her Ma about her and me going in behind the church and her Ma told her Da and her Da thumped her. I said that she would be OK, that I would go and hit her Da if he hit her again.

When we came down she ran away and I went back to where Fergus and Bill were. Mary was there waiting for me. She wanted to know if I had seen Stewart. Stewart usually drove up and down the plantation on a Sunday night but I hadn't seen him.

"He's no good," Bill says to her and she asked me to come up the road a bit to talk to her in private. We had just walked up a little bit when Stewart went flying past. He pulled in to the side and slid the wheels. Mary got all excited because she thought maybe he had stopped for her. But if he had been stopping for her he wouldn't have stopped as far away as that.

"What do I look like?" she says. "Is my hair all right? I –"

"You're all right," I say.

"He's not going to reverse up here," she says.

"He might," I say.

"You go and ask him the time to see if he says anything to you," she says. I didn't want to go at first but she kept on and on at me.

He was sitting in the big warm car. It smelt of polish and pig dung. Nice and warm. He had a big grin on.

"Mary wants to know the time," I say. He looked back.

"Tell her it's time she had a bit," he says and lets out a big loud laugh. She was trying not to look down our way.

"Is she any good?" he asks me.

"I'm not sure," I say. "I never tried her."

"You're the one that can get the girls," he says. "Jump in and we'll go for a drive and try and pick up something," he says. He liked me ever since one night we went to another village and I grabbed this girl and took her into a field. The thing was, when I was in the field he got the other one that was with her into the car. She was only about fourteen and he was twenty-four. But he didn't care. He had a good time. They went for a drive and didn't come back for ages. But I pretended that I had been in the field with the other one all the time although she got away not long after I had got her down.

"Jump in," he says.

"I better not go and leave Bill and Fergus," I say.

"Who the hell's Fergus?" he says, and looks at him sitting on the wall still dabbing his lip with his handkerchief although it wasn't bleeding any more.

"That little pansy," he says. "Bring him along for the laugh."

"A girl hit him," I say and Stewart nearly killed himself laughing.

We all got in. I felt sorry for Mary standing up there trying not to look at us. Stewart revved up the car and went off with a screech. You could smell the rubber from the tyres. Bill always enjoyed a ride in the car. He always got Stewart to go fast and Stewart enjoyed that.

"Put the shoe down boy," Bill says. "Let her have it."

Stewart laughed. He always laughed at Bill because he had been in a mental hospital. Fergus kept asking all sorts of questions, what sort of car it was and what speed it did and how many miles it did to the gallon. Stewart didn't seem to be too fond of him. He asked him if he knew anything about cars and Fergus says only what he had read.

"You're one of them boys that read a lot of books," Stewart says and he nudges me and winks.

We drove fast. The car just seemed to cut through between the hedges. No matter how fast we went Bill kept telling Stewart to put the shoe down. I thought the sun was down for the evening but suddenly it appeared really bright. I closed my eyes. The telegraph poles made little red flickers behind my eyelids. We crossed a little stream and the sun went down as fast as it came up. We were in another village. The girls were all supposed to be easy there. There was three women to every man because it was a dead village and all the men had left as soon as they could. We drove up to a pub with blue doors and windows. Stewart fancied a drink. Bill said he would like one too. Fergus said that he thought he wouldn't bother. He would take a walk and explore the village.

"There's bugger all to explore," Stewart says. "Two or three houses and a pub. That's all there is here. But maybe you want to get out and walk home." Fergus was embarrassed and he just sat where he was. Stewart got out and went to the door. It was a long time opening and when it did open, it just opened a little bit. Then he went inside.

"They might not let him have any on a Sunday," Bill says.

"What are you talking about?" I say. "That pub does more trade on a Sunday than any other day."

"Balls," Bill says. "You think you know everything. You're like this eejit here." And he looks at Fergus.

"There, what did I say?" I say. Stewart was coming out with a big brown bag.

It was strong beer he had. I had had it before. The first time I had it was one night Stewart took me there and we had a box of cream cakes with us too and we got this girl to come into the car and she had a nice frock on and she sat on the cream cakes and then I was sick all over her.

"Remember the first time we had this beer?" Stewart says.

"I remember OK," I say. He gave us all a bottle. Fergus said that he didn't think he would have any and Stewart told him to get it down him. He told him to be a man and not a bloody pansy. So he had to drink it. Stewart made him drink the next bottle too and the next one. He had no bother telling Bill to drink it. He loved it and he was always finished before any of us. He liked getting drunk. I always thought I would stop before I was really drunk but if it was there I never knew when I was and when I wasn't. I felt as if we were looking through glass. Then I felt as if we were moving and we weren't.

"I think I'm drunk," I say. "It's strong stuff." It was good to be drunk too. Sometimes Bill and me would get a bottle of beer between us and I would go up the plantation and pretend I was drunk. I think the girls like it.

We drove out the road to where the girls from the village usually were. We turned down the windows ready for them. But it was a bad night for they wouldn't stop even for Stewart's car. Stewart said they were a snotty lot and we should just grab one and pull her into the car. Stewart wanted Fergus to do it. He said he wanted to see Fergus in action. Fergus seemed to be a bit quiet for a while. Then suddenly he starts singing. He sang some kind of odd song about a prince. His voice was really funny and we were killing ourselves laughing. He put out his arms and held the last note for ages. When he had finished we all clapped. That got him onto another song. Then he lay back for a while with his eyes closed.

"The world is going round," he says. "It is spinning towards the sun. Do you know how many light years the sun is away from us? Forget that. You are all natural country boys. You are great. I wish I wasn't so inhibited. I would love a little girl. There is no point in pretending that I wouldn't."

"Here's one coming now," Bill says. "You go out and grab her." Fergus tried to open the car door but he couldn't manage it with his eyes closed. Then he opened them and saw the girl that was coming along. She was a little dark girl with a pretty face. Fergus got out and stood on the pavement in front of her. She went to go to one side of him and he made a grab for her and fell on his mouth and nose. I got out and tried to lift him. At first I thought he was crying. Then I realized he was laughing.

"Don't move me," he says. "Don't move me as I am happy." As soon as I got back in again Stewart starts off the car and we drove away leaving him lying there.

"We can't leave him," I say.

"We'll go back for him later," Stewart says.

We drove off the main road and along a flat little bumpy road. We could see the sun again.

"Jesus, look at the lovely little calf," Stewart shouts. There was an old farmer coming out of a field and this little calf was following him. Stewart jams on the brakes and puts it into reverse. We got up level with them. Stewart turns down the window. The calf was red and white. It had little thin legs and a nice little head.

"It's lovely," I say to the farmer. The farmer had the brim of his hat pulled down over his eyes and he was smiling.

"It's a pet," he says, and pushed his hat further back on his head. He had nice smiley eyes too. The calf nudged at his arms with its nose. He stroked it with two big rough fingers between its eyes.

"How much will you take for it?" Stewart asks him.

"Oh, I wouldn't sell it for love or money," the farmer says. "Its poor mother died and I have been feeding it with the bottle." He stroked it again. "It follows me everywhere." He was proud.

"It must give you a lot of bother," Stewart says.

"You're no bother to me," he says to the little calf. "You're my little girl, aren't you?"

"Will you take a tenner for it?" Stewart says.

"It would break my heart to get rid of it," the farmer says. Stewart gets out and walks around it. The farmer stands close to it. Stewart comes back and leans against the car and looks at it. Round its nose was all white.

"I'll take it off your hands for fifteen pounds," Stewart says.

"No," the farmer says. "If it was any other calf I would take your offer. But not with this one."

"Come on, come on," Stewart says. "You're a farmer. You

need the money the same as anybody else." The farmer laughs.

"Money couldn't buy it," he says.

"Come on," Stewart says. "What good's a bloody calf to you without a mother. It only wastes time." The farmer looks up round the sky as if he wanted to get away or something and the sky was holding him in. The calf snuggled into the palm of his hand.

"She wants her milk," he says, and goes to walk away. Stewart steps out in front of him.

"Is my offer not good enough," he says. "Is my money no good." He pushes the farmer a little bit with his shoulder. The farmer staggers and laughs. Then he gets right in front of him and doesn't let him past. The farmer looks down at the calf as if he was asking what he could do. "You'll sell it to me," Stewart says.

"I would any other calf," the farmer says.

"Come on Stewart. He likes it," I say.

"What are you picking on an old man for?" Bill says. Stewart looks up and his big brown face has gone a kind of red.

"You shut up," he says.

"Who's going to make me shut up?" Bill says.

The farmer looks at us as if he was asking us to pity him. "Come on," he says to Stewart. "The fun's over."

Stewart pushes him back. "The fun's only beginning," he says. "I'll ask you one more time. Are you going to sell me that calf?"

The farmer gives a little laugh. "No lad," he says. "I couldn't part with her now." Stewart drew off and sent the old man into the thick hedge. The little calf takes a few shaky steps backwards.

"Keep your bloody calf," Stewart says, and jumps into the car. A little bit of blood is coming out of the old man's nose.

The calf looks as if it isn't too sure what to do. Stewart starts the car.

"You can't leave him," I say. But he doesn't listen to me. He skids the tyres on the grass and we almost touch the farmer's feet going past.

We drove in silence for a long way. I was thinking about the old farmer and the little calf and I was nearly crying. I took a big deep breath and felt a bit better. It was Bill that spoke first.

"You should try somebody your own age next time," he says.

"You keep your trap closed or you'll get the same," Stewart says. "Nobody'll tell me my money's not good enough."

"He didn't want to sell it – that's all," I say.

"Whose side are you on?" Stewart says. I said nothing.

"Just because you've got money doesn't mean you own everything," Bill says. "I think you're suffering from a complex. I think you need treatment."

Stewart pulls into the side and stops. "You say that again," Stewart says.

"I think you need treatment," Bill says.

"Nobody tells me I'm mental," Stewart says.

"You need your head looking at," Bill says.

"Get out and say that," Stewart says. Bill opened the door and gets out and then Stewart gets out too. He was big – about a foot bigger than Bill. Bill stood there with his big head solid on his thick neck. But the rest of his body wasn't too well built.

"You need your head looking at all right," he says.

"I don't want to hit anybody that's mental," Stewart says.

"Try it," Bill says. "Come on and try it."

Stewart put out his hand to slap Bill on the cheek. But Bill was fast and he hit Stewart a crack on the wrist. It hurt Stewart but he didn't want to show it.

"Come on," Stewart says. "I'm not going to hit a chap who's sick in the mind."

Bill had his fists up all the time, ready. Stewart stuck his hands in his pocket. "I could make mincemeat of you if I wanted to," he says. "But I won't hit somebody that's mental." Stewart got into the car. "Come on," he says. "I'm not fighting."

Bill gets into the car too. "You're scared," he says. Stewart straightened up to the little mirror. Bill had cooled down now and he was making faces behind Stewart's back. Stewart saw him in the mirror and laughed because Bill could make some really funny faces.

"Right," Bill says. "Right, driver, take us to pick up the pansy." Stewart didn't like to be called the driver but he said nothing.

Fergus wasn't where we left him. We found him further up the road with a little group of girls around him. I got out and went over to them. Fergus was sitting in the ditch. There was a slight little cut on his chin and another one on his nose. It's an odd thing but it seemed to make him better-looking. The girls were asking him what England was like.

"Did you get that accent there?" one of the girls asked him.

"It's a combination," Fergus says.

"Talk," another of the girls says. "I love to hear you talking." Fergus didn't seem too shy either.

"I can't think what to say," he says. They all giggled and tried to speak the same way as him. Stewart beeps the horn of the car.

"Do you want to come for a drive?" he says to the girls. They look round at him and then back to Fergus.

"There are lots of lovely girls in this village," Fergus says. And they all roared with laughter.

"Do you talk like that all the time?" one of them asks him.

Fergus did more or less talk like that all the time except I think he was putting on a little bit of an American accent. He talked like some of those blokes you get on the TV. Fergus looked up and saw me. Then he stood up and tried to introduce me.

"This is Moren, this is Sylvia and this is Diana." Then he couldn't think of the last one's name. "I'm sorry," he says. "Your name has slipped my mind for the moment." She pretended to be angry.

"You remember everybody's name only mine," she says. And she kind of pretended to cry.

"I'm really sorry," Fergus says. "It has just slipped my mind at present. And it was a nice name too – Briddie," he says. "Briddie, that's it. Briddie, this is my friend Johnny." The girls all looked at me. They asked me where I was from and when I told them I was from the next village they didn't want to know.

"He has awful good manners," one of the girls says. Fergus looks at his watch.

"Well, I'm afraid I better be going," he says.

The girls all said, "Ahhhhh." "What about a kiss before you go?" one of them says. Fergus didn't seem shy at all. He went round them all and gave them all a little kiss on the cheek. When we got into the car they all stood and looked in. But they didn't look at us. It was just Fergus. And they waved at Fergus and threw kisses at him and he waved at them until they were out of sight.

"Did you get anything?" Stewart says.

"They are lovely girls," Fergus says. "They're not that type."

"They're all that type," Stewart says.

"They seemed to like you," I say.

"I liked them," he says.

"Are you going to see them again?" I ask him.

"I was going to ask them if I could come over and see them," he says. "But I didn't know them long enough for that really."

"It shows you what a few bottles of beer can do for you," Bill says.

"I must admit, it gives you courage," Fergus says.

"Is there any more left?" Stewart asks me. I looked in the big brown bag. There was a lot of empty bottles but down at the bottom there was two that hadn't been opened. We all agreed that Fergus should have them both. He said no, that we should divide them equal. But we insisted. It was good to see him doing so well. All the way we talked about the girls.

When we got to our village there wasn't so many girls around. We got out and sat on the wall up the plantation. Two or three girls went past and we shouted at them but we didn't try to catch them. But we tried to get Fergus to go after them. He said he would but he would wait until he saw a girl he fancied. He didn't bother with any of them until Mary came along then the eyes nearly popped out of his head. You could see it plain.

"Grab her," Stewart says. But it seemed like he was in a kind of a dream.

"Hallo Mary," I say. She blushed and walked past a bit and stopped.

"Can I talk to you for a minute, Johnny?" she says.

"I think it's you she's after," Stewart says. I went up to her.

"I thought you weren't coming back," she says.

"We only went for a drive," I say.

"I suppose Stewart didn't mention me," she says.

"Well . . ." I say.

"He didn't Johnny, now did he?"

"Well he came back here, didn't he?" I say.

"Do you think he came back to see me?" she says. Then

Stewart came up. He put his arm around Mary and she didn't know what to do. She didn't move away.

"How's my sweet Mary?" he says.

"You're only saying that," she says. "You say things like that to every girl."

"Johnny, do I ever say anything nice to other girls?" Stewart says. Mary kind of lay against him.

"I never heard you," I say.

Poor Mary. Big Stewart – his big brown face, his big bones and Mary lying against him. And he doesn't care. But she wants him. She wants him more than anything. That's all she lives for. But he doesn't care. He's got money and that big car. He's got his Ma who worships the ground he walks on. He does nothing. I was up in their big house too. A big farmhouse smelling of milk and meat and a big fire. And all the men out on the farm doing the work for them. And Stewart lies with his feet out and does nothing and she brings him cups of tea and sticks pound notes into his pocket, and cigarettes. When he was younger, just after his father died and before the money came to him, he went and lay across the railway lines until she came down and gave him the money for a motor bicycle.

"Will you do something for me, and then we'll go for a little ride," Stewart says to her.

"What is it?" Mary asks.

"Never mind," Stewart says. "Will you do it?"

"All right," she says.

"Right," Stewart says. "Do you see that little pimple-faced pansy there? You get into the back seat with him and see what he can do. You see if there is any of the man in him or not. Give him a bit of a cuddle and kiss and we'll see how he gets on."

"I couldn't do that Stewart," she says.

"That's all right," Stewart says. "We'll not be going for a

drive then." And he goes to walk away. Mary catches him by the coat.

"I'll do it Stewart," she says. "Then we'll go for a drive on our own."

We went down and got into the car. Bill, me and Stewart got into the front seat and Fergus in the back.

"Where will I sit?" Mary says.

"Where would you like to sit?" Stewart says and he winks at her.

"I would like to sit in the back," she says.

Fergus was red and sweating and he kept looking at her. He moved far over towards his door to give her room.

"Don't worry, I'll not bite you," Mary says. But Fergus stayed close to his door. He stuck his hands in his pockets and then brought them out again. He didn't know what to do with them. There was plenty of room in the back seat but Mary sat close to him.

"I wish I was in the back," Stewart says.

"Do you want to change places?" Fergus says.

"Give her a squeeze," Bill says. "Go on, get in there. Put your arm around her."

"You're not scared of me," Mary says. Fergus didn't know what to say. He gave a kind of laugh.

"Not really," he says. Mary caught one of his hands.

"You're sweating, love," she says.

"Maybe we shouldn't be here," Stewart says. Mary took Fergus's hand and put it round her shoulder.

"Let's be friends," she says. Fergus went to look at his watch but he couldn't because his arm was round her shoulder.

"You probably smell beer on me," he says. Mary put her mouth close to his.

"That's it," Stewart says. "There's going to be a long drive for you." But he pretended that he wasn't really talking to Mary. Mary gave Fergus a little smack on the cheek and put an arm around him. It was getting very dark and you could hardly see what was going on in the dark. But you could hear the noises. Fergus gave a kind of nervous giggle every now and then.

"Keep it going," Stewart kept saying. "Yes, it'll be a long drive."

"Stop buggering about and get in there," Bill kept saying. There was heavy breathing. Fergus's was real but Mary was just putting it on. You could hear them moving about all over the back of the car. Sometimes you could hear their skin rubbing hard against the leather covering on the seat.

After we got out, Stewart and her drove away. Fergus was shaking like anything. He didn't speak for a long time and then when he did start he would talk about nothing but Mary. He said that he had never had an experience like that before. He said that she stuck her tongue down his throat and everything. Bill thought that was funny. He said that if she had done that to him he would have hit her a slap on the mouth. Fergus said Bill didn't understand. The experience had opened his eyes and now he knew what life was about. He was thinking of not going to Oxford now. He told us about her putting her hand down his trousers too.

I couldn't tell him. I couldn't tell him that she was having him on. Bill told him but he didn't believe him.

"She's a prick teaser," Bill says. "She just done that to please Stewart." Fergus just laughed, and said that it was something he wouldn't forget for a while. Then before he left us he told us something that he had been wanting to tell us all along. She wanted him to take her to the dance the following Friday. I knew about the dance. It was in the church hall. Old Mrs Reed's daughter was going to America and for some reason they were giving a farewell dance for her. Her daughter was called Birdie. She had always been called that. Nobody knew why and nobody knew why she was going to America or wherever she was going, because old Mrs Reed was pretty old and Birdie would be taking over the post office when the old woman went. Folk expected her to go any time. She never has no trouble with her heart or anything but if you worked her age out she should have gone long ago.

Fergus thought he was in love. He had never felt like this before. But he was worried. He thought Mary might not like him if she saw him in daylight. I told him that she had seen him in daylight, but he still wasn't happy. I told him that he shouldn't bother too much about her, that there was plenty of girls in the village. But he said that he could never feel the same about another girl. Bill told him that that was balls, but it didn't make any difference. He was still worried about something. In the end he came out with it. We were standing below a street-lamp at the time.

"Tell me Johnny," he says. "Would you say you are my friend?"

"I am," I say.

"Will you tell me the truth?" he says.

"Well, I'll try," I say.

"Hurry up," Bill says. "We can't arse around here all night." Then that put him off and he couldn't ask me whatever it was. We left and went up the street a bit and then he came after us.

"You'll tell me the truth," he says. Bill walked on. He waited until Bill was out of hearing distance, then he says, "I won't be upset, as long as you tell me the truth."

"What is it?" I say.

"Do you think I'm good-looking?" he says.

I stood there. I didn't know what to say. His greasy nose

and his weak looking eyes and that pimply face. But it wasn't that so much. I mean he had eyes and a nose and a mouth the same as everybody else, but there was something wrong with him. I tried to figure it out. Maybe his eyes seemed to be too far up his forehead or something. No, it wasn't that. Maybe there was too big a space between his nose and his upper lip. I'm not sure. All in, he had everything but they didn't seem to be the right length apart.

"I know what you are going to say," he says. "I can take it."

"There's nobody all that good-looking around here," I say.

"You are softening the blow," he says.

"I reckon you're as good-looking as anybody else," I say.

"Do you mean that?" he says. I said I did and he walked further up the street with me. After we were up past Pot Stick Street, he asks me, "Can I ask you something else?" I said he could. "Maybe you think I'm silly," he says. "But do you think my breath smells?"

"I never really smelt it," I say. I had to stop and he breathed into my face. It did smell a bit. It kind of smelt of sour milk and onions. And beer too.

"It doesn't smell too bad," I say. He cupped his hand over his mouth and over his nose and breathed out.

"I can't really tell," he says.

"I would never worry about a thing like that," I say.

"It's different for you," he says. "You are natural."

"Thanks for being a good friend," he says before he turns to go home.

Ma was kicking up a fuss when I got in. Bill was already home and she had smelt the beer from him. She wanted to know what Da was going to do about it.

Da said, "What can you do?"

"You could thump some sense into them," Ma says. But Da was too interested in the TV. There was a service on. It showed you a lot of people singing hymns. It made the TV look like a goldfish bowl. All you could see was these big mouths coming up to the glass.

"They're great singers these people," Da says.

"If we had these two boys singing in the church choir," Ma says. "But they would rather go out drinking on a Sunday."

"If you would shut your mouth for a while," Bill says.

"Don't tell me to shut my mouth," Ma says. "You're not too big yet for me to hammer some sense into you."

Bill got up and kicked a chair across the room.

"Sit down, Bill," I say.

"Wreck the house," Ma says. "I don't care, you have to live in it as well as me." Da was pretending that nothing was happening.

"This bloody place is sending me mad," Bill shouts. "That's why I'm locked up half the time. That's why I need treatment."

"It's the drink talking," Ma says. Bill hit the chair another kick and one of the legs came off. Da still pretended nothing was happening.

"It's the drink that's sending you mad," Ma says. "If you would be like them nice boys there and go to church." She pointed to the TV. There was a row of nice boys with short haircuts and suits on and collars and ties. They were all licking their lips. "If you went to church and prayed you might get better," Ma says.

"Shut your mouth," Bill says. "You're driving me out of my mind. You're sending me back into the hospital. I can't stand it."

"Sit down," Ma says. "Sit down and listen to me. If you had listened to me when you were younger you never would have been in the hospital in the first place." Bill put his hands over his face.

"Get away," he shouts. "Get away or I'll do something. I can stand no more."

"Get up to bed Ma and let him be," I say.

Ma picked up the chair and brought it over to Bill. She put it on his knee. Bill caught hold of it and threw it. It hit the far wall and two more legs came off it.

"Wreck the place," Ma shouts. "Go on, wreck the place." Da goes over and turns the TV up really loud.

"It's the drink," Ma says. "It's odd what drink can do." Suddenly Bill got up and flew at her. She fell against the wall and he got her round the throat. She let out a kind of scream and fell on the floor. Bill was mad. He was letting out a mad kind of scream. Then Ma nearly got up and I thought it was all right. But no. He got her down again.

"Let go," Da was saying. "Let her go." Then Ma let out a kind of scream and Da and me tried to pull him off. He was strong when he was like that. His arms were flying all over the place and two or three times he hit Ma on the face. In the end we got hold of him and made him sit back on the sofa. He didn't speak. He just sat there with his hands over his face. Ma just lay there pretending to be dead. Then I reckon she had held her breath long enough and she started to breathe again. But they were little quick shaky breaths. Da tried to pick her up but every time he tried she let out a loud moan.

It was easy enough to get Bill to go to bed. "Come on Bill," I say and he got up and walked up the stairs with me. He just got up and walked up the stairs with me. He just lay on the top of the bed with his clothes on and I had to undress him. It was as if he didn't know what was happening to him. When I got him right into bed he just lay there with his eyes staring. He must have thought I was the nurse or something because he said "Leave me nurse. Leave me." I sat at the bottom of the bed for a while looking at him.

Then I heard Da bring Ma up to bed. She was saying that she couldn't walk right.

I sat with Bill until I was nearly asleep. For a while he talked a lot of nonsense. "When I paint these pictures I can see all sorts of women in them," he says. "There's blood running out of them. I did that. I can see everything in bright colours. Bright coloured lights too."

"You just go to sleep," I say, and I pull the blankets up under his chin.

"You want to smother me," he says and he pulls them down quick. Then for a while I thought he had gone to sleep, but he hadn't.

"I see the colours all going into one another," he says. "Coloured stars all getting brighter and brighter." Then he starts to sweat and opens his eyes. "I'm starting to swell," he says. "Stop it. Stop me from getting bigger and bigger. I'm getting heavier too. God – Christ – Stop it happening." He let out one scream and then he really did go to sleep. I lay down on the bed beside him just to make sure.

Halfway through the night I got up and went into my own bed. I lay and thought about Bill. I wondered what was going on in his head. I thought maybe I was the same as him because I had odd things going round in my head too. I had an odd kind of dream while I was awake. I dreamt there was this big fire in the factory where Da worked. All the linen had caught light and everybody was there. There was Jack Robinson, Sam Kerr, Ma, Da, Bill, Fergus and everybody I could think of. Then the fire was over and everybody was lying there with their eyes all burnt. The fire had burnt their skin to a hard crust over their eyes. Then Fergus's Da came along and pushed his toe into each eye. The crust broke and a trickle of blood was coming from each eye.

I sat up and put the light on to prove to myself that the

dream wasn't true. But it was with me strong. I tried to think about something else, but every time the thing came back to me. I could almost see the dream hanging over me. For some reason I thought if I washed my face it would go away. I got up and went into the bathroom. The bathroom was next door to Bill's room. I went quietly not to waken him. But when I was just about to open the door I heard noise coming from his room. I opened his door slowly and looked in. He was lying on his belly crying like anything. I went and put my arms around him and told him it was all right. But he said nothing. He just kept on crying.

The next thing I knew it was morning and I had been lying with him all night. But he wasn't crying now. He was just lying there staring at the ceiling. I spoke to him but he didn't answer. He just lay there as if he was dead but he still had his eyes open.

When I got downstairs Ma was going on about him. She said she would have to get the doctor for him, that he was a danger. All she had was a little scratch above her eye but she said that she was sore all over. And she said that when Bill had his hands around her throat she thought she was dead. She said that he had cut off her wind and that stopped the blood from going to the brain. So she might have a brain haemorrhage.

"He doesn't seem to be too good this morning," I say.

"That's the way it is with him," Ma says. "One minute he's up and the next minute he's down. Why can't he be like other people. Sometimes I think he just does it for badness."

Ma went on about all sorts of things. She said there was never illness like that when she was young. "You went out and did a good day's work and when you came in, if you talked back to your Ma you would get a thump along the ear that you wouldn't forget for a while." She said that Da was too soft with us, that he had no control. Then she started going on and on about us drinking the night before. She went on about that until Fergus called for me. He was still on about that X-ray. He had all sorts of papers with him. A medical card, letters to say what injections he had had, and judging by the papers he had every injection you could have. Ma said you could never be too sure, that you were wise to get an X-ray. Then if there was a hole in your lungs you knew about it. She told Fergus not to worry, that they had some of the best doctors in the world in the big new hospital in the town. She said that maybe Fergus would think she was old-fashioned but she believed in faith. Fergus said "Indeed."

There was only one bus into the town and it took ages coming and it took ages getting into the town. It went round half the countryside and picked up nobody. Well, it picked up one old man who kept making a noise with his nose. It was a kind of snort. The first time he did it I thought he was just blowing his nose, but then after that he kept doing it all the time. I couldn't stop laughing but Fergus didn't laugh at all. He pretended not to notice it. I kind of enjoyed it in an odd way. I wanted to go up to the front of the bus to see how he did it.

When we got to the town I wanted fish and chips but Fergus wouldn't stop. We had to go straight to the hospital to keep the appointment. But we could have had fish and chips because there was hundreds of people waiting to be X-rayed. Most of them were women. There was something wrong with them all. Some of them had big bandages round their legs. Some had big patches on their eyes. You would think to look at the place that somebody had come in and gone mad on them. We sat down beside a man that looked more normal than the rest of them. He kept looking at Fergus.

"You wait for ages in these places," he says.

"Indeed," Fergus says.

"I've been waiting here two hours now," he says. He looks at Fergus's watch. "It's time I had some dinner," he says. "Cold pigeon and mashed potatoes with greens. What do you think of that? For breakfast I had two kippers and a big mug of tea. I like breakfast. Well, I don't like breakfast more than any other meal. I had a good meal last night. A little bit of steak, not too thick with a little rim of fat round it. You see you rub salt into the fat and just let it see the pan. Then you spread brown crispy onions over it and have a few roast potatoes with it. Never overcook steak."

"I prefer steak rare," Fergus says.

"Look at these people here," the man says and he waved his hand around the waiting-room. "Half of them are dying on their feet. Look at them. Just look at them." Fergus looks round. "Half of them are dying. Kidney trouble. Bowel trouble, God knows what else. That's because they don't eat the right food." A girl with a white coat on came out and called a woman in. The man went on. "I'm next but never mind that. They don't eat. Look at them. What I like best is a pork chop – not fried, no. Grilled with a little salt on the fat and then add a few mild herbs and plenty of pepper. Then you get the juice from the chop and make a nice sauce. You get an apple and cut it up and stew it and put a couple of cloves in it and add a few other things to taste. You know it's an art. A little bit of what you've got in the kitchen. Well then, if you've a log fire you stick two or three potatoes in that and let them burn black. Then bring them out and smother them with butter."

"It sounds very nice," Fergus says. The man looked at Fergus quick, as if Fergus had just called him a liar or something.

"What do you mean 'It's nice'?" he says.

A few people were pushed past in wheelchairs and on

stretchers. "Look at them," the man says. "Bloody hell. If they would eat. Look at that old girl. She needs a good meal." He pointed to a thin woman who was being pushed by in a wheelchair. "Rat's brains. That's what that woman needs. That would make her walk. But do you know, it's laziness that's wrong with half of these people." The girl with a white coat came out again and looked at a card then went back in. The man got up. Then when she went back in he sat down as if he was prepared to sit there for ever.

"What's wrong with you?" he says to Fergus.

"I'm getting a chest X-ray," he says. The man looked at him thoughtfully.

"Are you coughing up blood?" he asks.

"Not really," Fergus says.

"What about your breathing?" the man says. "Is it all right?"

"Well, I get a bit exhausted at times," Fergus says.

"I thought that to look at you," the man says. "Perforated lungs. That's what it is." The man considered the conversation closed from then and went back to food.

"I like nice little trout. That's what you need about seven o'clock at night. Or maybe a herring with a few drops of lemon on it."

"Do you know much about the lungs?" Fergus asks him.

"Now," the man says. "Now, I know about more than the lungs. I come here every three months and get X-rayed all over. They can't refuse you know. It's this new system."

The girl in the white coat came out again and called him in. But he didn't go straight in when she called out his name. He stood up and looked around at all the people in the waiting-room. "You're next. After me," he says. Then he pointed to another woman. "You'll be after her," he says. "And you can sort the rest out among yourselves."

"He's interesting," Fergus says.

"He went on a bit anyway," I say.

Fergus expected them to tell him that he had cancer straightaway, but they didn't. They said they would send a report to his doctor. Fergus was worried about that. He thought they knew but didn't want to tell him. He thought the doctor might just tell his Mum and keep it from him.

"If you've got it, you've got it. There's no need to worry," I say. I was fed up with all that waiting and everything. And Fergus wouldn't even buy me fish and chips after we left the hospital. Everywhere he seen he said he would wait until we found somewhere cleaner. In the end I went and bought my own. Then he started going on again about taking Mary to the dance the next Friday night. He said he wanted something to make his breath smell nice. We went to this chemist's and Fergus wouldn't ask for anything because it was girls behind the counter. The next chemist we went into had girls behind the counter too. We ended up with two toothbrushes and three bars of soap before we got this chemist with a man behind the counter. Then Fergus didn't like to ask him either. In the end he says, "Have you got anything that gives you mouth freshness?"

"Do you clean your teeth regular?" the chemist asks. Fergus said he did and the chemist asked him what exactly was wrong.

"Sometimes I get this bad taste in my mouth," Fergus says.

"It might be your mouth," the chemist says. Fergus was about to leave when the chemist called him back. He was kind of laughing. "Here son. Try this." He reached Fergus this little bottle. It said Gold Spot on it. "You just dab a little bit of this on your tongue," the chemist says. "That'll help you to get the girls. Anything else you want?" The chemist was enjoying himself and we came out with a big bag of stuff. He had stuff that you put under your arms, stuff that you put between your legs and stuff you bathed in. And he had stuff that you put on your hair to give it a silky look.

"You could nearly start a shop of your own in the village," I say.

He made me promise that I wouldn't tell anybody that he had bought all that stuff, but I'm sure people knew because you could smell him all the way home in the bus. The chemist had made him put some perfume behind his ears too.

I was looking forward to telling Bill about it when I got home but he was still in bed. Sometimes we had a good laugh about things like that, but when he stayed in bed all day you couldn't talk to him. Ma was sitting downstairs at the window.

"Look at them nice happy women going down past," she says. I said nothing. I went straight up to Bill.

"Are you feeling OK?" I ask him. He didn't answer. He said nothing for a long time.

"It'll go away," I say.

"It'll never go away," he says. "What's behind all this? What makes you think?"

"I'm not sure," I say.

"Why am I lying here in this still room?" he says. "Sometimes I can see animals coming through the air. Big animals made of flame. Where do they come from? Why do I feel like this? I'm simple. I can see every thought that goes through my mind. I can see the whole thing moving. Sometimes a black bar comes down and won't let me think any more."

"What about them tablets you had? Didn't them help you last time you thought like this?" I say.

"I've got to go through with it," he says. "I've got to find out what's behind it. Here's three thoughts coming now. I can see them. They're running along little white rails."

"Do you want me to get the doctor?" I say. But he pays no attention.

"Three thoughts," he says. "I'll let one through. Yes, I've got it. I thought I would drink a glass of milk. But I don't want a glass of milk. I'll just let that thought go on into the sky."

I went down and got a glass of milk but he didn't want it.

I sat with him until it was nearly dark. Sometimes he talked about things and sometimes he didn't. I just wanted him to get better. Maybe he knows more than me and maybe he doesn't, but it doesn't matter. I just want him to get better. He wasn't always the way he is now. When we were young we used to fish and we used to catch trout too. Sometimes we used to go and build hide-outs. We had real fires in them too. Bill was the one. He was always able to steal some of Da's cigarettes. It was good lying looking through the cool ferns in the summer evenings – smoking and Bill showing me how to inhale. Oh Bill.

He didn't get better. He got worse and worse. Sometimes he would just thump his head against the pillow. And sometimes he would cry. Not an ordinary cry. An odd cry, as if the tears were being squeezed out of his brain. I wasn't much good. I said little prayers but maybe I didn't say them right. Da was no good either. He always came up after he got back from work and said something stupid like "Just try and pull yourself together. Come down and watch the TV and you'll forget all about it." One time when Bill was crying that odd cry Da came up with two Aspros and a cup of tea and told Bill that if he got that down him he would be OK. He said he could swear by Aspros and a cup of tea. It would cure anything. Bill took them. I think he just more or less took them because he didn't know what he was doing.

Fergus called up for me two or three times but I didn't go down. I couldn't leave Bill because I love him more than anything. Maybe it's because he's my brother – maybe it's not. Even when we were younger and he looked at me with that big head and them big eyes I felt like crying. But he was good fun. We did all sorts of things. We had an old shed and we put peat in it and lamps that we made ourselves and kept the hens in there and they laid day and night. Then other folk discovered that idea and did the same thing and called it "deep litter". Bill had one hen. It was all brown except for two or three white feathers. I remember it died one Sunday and Bill and me had a funeral. He made a grave for it too and put flowers on it.

When Fergus came up Ma always asked him in and I could hear her talking to him in the kitchen.

"Maybe I better go down for the doctor," I say to Bill but he didn't answer. Ma said it was up to me when I told her that I thought I better go. She said that she never had nothing but trouble ever since we were born.

The doctor came up with me straight away. I liked him. He was nice to Bill. Ma stopped him in the hall and told him about Bill hitting her but he said nothing. He came up into the room and left his little case down and just looked at Bill. Bill was losing a lot of sweat. "How are you feeling son?" he says. Bill sort of smiled then closed his eyes. The doctor went and took Bill's wrist and looked at his watch. Then he got up.

"We better have him in the hospital again," he says. "I think he's got a little bit of a fever on top of everything else." Then he left. There was nothing to do but sit and wait for the ambulance to come. Then there would be a crowd round it watching Bill going away. I said nothing to Bill while we waited. Maybe he knew and maybe he didn't.

They came straight up the stairs. It was two men that had come to take him away before. Da was home and he followed them up.

"I think it's the flu," he says.

The ambulance men didn't say nothing. They just put Bill on the red stretcher. You could hear all the excited children that had gathered around outside. Some of the children were game enough to go right up close to the stretcher. Ma was really stupid. She came out and asked the ambulance men if they wanted a cup of tea.

One of them got into the back where Bill was. They asked Da if anybody wanted to go into the hospital with him but Da said he didn't see any point. But I went. I just got into the front and we went away nice and smooth. The children were really excited then, and you could see all the women peeping out from behind the curtains as we drove down through the estate.

I didn't like the hospital. I had been there before. There was a lot of really crazy people there. They wheeled Bill down this long corridor and all these people followed us and tried to touch me. You couldn't make out what they were saying either.

Bill was in a big ward with about twenty beds in it, but there was only two or three people in the beds. The rest of the people were scattered all over the place. A group of them sat at a long table making stools or something and some of them sat on their own. They just sat swaying from side to side all the time. One chap came right up to Bill in bed and caught him by the hand. I'm not sure whether he wanted to shake hands with Bill or not. A big fat nurse came up and caught him by the scruff of the neck and pushed him away across the ward. Most of the nurses were big fat girls but there was one nice one that came up and asked me all sorts of questions about Bill. She seen that Bill was too hot and she pulled the bedclothes down a bit.

I sat for a while and when I got outside it was really dark and you could hear all sorts of noises coming from the big grounds. Walking through those grounds is a bit like being in a field with a bull in it. If you start running the bull is sure to come after you, but if you just walk slow it thinks you're not scared and it just stays there. I didn't walk too fast. I didn't look back either.

Further up the drive I seen something moving among the bushes, but I kept on walking. Then when I got right up, there was a man standing there. My heart was pounding up through my ears. You got all sorts of people in that hospital. There was one man there because he slit a nun's throat and there was another man there because he strangled his little girl with a cheese-cutter. He got out once but they didn't put him in jail, they put him in the hospital. Bill told me about last time he was in there he met a doctor who cut off a woman's breasts for no reason. Bill said he was a nice man.

The man walked across the drive in front of me but I walked on.

"Hallo," I say.

"Good night," he says. And I walked on past him. Then I heard his steps behind me. "Just a minute," he says. I stopped but I was scared to look round. He caught up with me.

"Hallo," I say.

"Are you a patient?" he says.

"No it's my brother," I say. "He's a schizophrenic." He stood looking at me with his hands in his pockets.

"I see," he says. He seemed to think it over for a bit.

"Well, that's OK. I've got to keep an eye on some of these lads."

"Are you a kind of a watchman then," I say.

"No, no," he says, kind of offhand. "I'm a doctor."

"It must be a hard job making some of them people better," I say.

"Oh no," he says. "Not really. We'll have about twenty or

thirty of them better by the end of the week. We use different methods you know. Oh yes."

"Bill got electric last time he was in here" I say.

"Interesting, interesting," the man says and rubbed his chin. "What's your brother's name?"

"Bill," I say.

"Well, we'll see to it that Bill gets good treatment. Perhaps we should try a different method of treatment on him this time. Do you know there's more neurotic people outside this hospital than in. And the funny thing about it is that we have got to make them ready for the outside world."

"Bill says there's a lot of neurotic people outside too," I say.

"Would you like to come in and have treatment yourself?" he says.

"Well, maybe I'm not too bad," I say.

He looks at me kind of sideways. "Mmm," he says, and keeps on looking at me.

"I'm sure there's plenty of people to treat," I say.

"We still can't get enough," he says. "We advertise in the newspapers and all over the place to try and get patients but still we can't fill the beds up."

"That's odd," I say. "Last time Bill was in they had to let him out early because they needed the bed."

"Are you nervous?" he says. "I see that you keep fiddling with your fingers. If you need treatment come in and I'll fix you up."

"I think I'm OK," I say. He let out a loud laugh.

"That's what they all say." He pointed to the hospital. "Look at that building full of neurotic people and they all say they are OK. I'll have to treat all those people tomorrow and they'll say they are all OK. Look, if you need treatment you have just got to tell me. You might as well have it while you can. We are going to pull this place down soon."

"What for?" I say.

"What for?" he says. "Why do you think? We need the room."

"I better go," I say.

"Don't hurry away," he says. "Don't bury your head in the sand. Come and get treated like everybody else." I start walking away and he walks with me. Then suddenly he looks at his watch.

"I must go," he says. "I have got things to do. I am sorry. You'll have to come back another day." He turns and hurries towards the hospital. Then I heard a loud scream and I hurry out onto the road.

It wasn't a good place to stand outside the hospital to get a lift because everybody knew it was a mental hospital and they were scared to stop in case you had just got out from there. I kept on walking and hitching at the same time. All the cars seemed to slow down and for a minute I felt good because I thought they were going to stop for me. But they didn't. It was ages before one stopped. At first I didn't recognize who it was. Then when he opened the door the light came on and I could see that it was Fergus's Dad. He had the two big dogs in the back seat. I had never seen him close up before. He was wearing a corduroy cap and a corduroy jacket. He had big thick black eyebrows and big black eyes too. He wasn't in the least like Fergus. He had dark skin and a big red mouth with a pipe stuck between his teeth. He said nothing. He seemed not to look at me either. I didn't like to speak either. I was kind of scared of him. So I just stroked one of the dogs. Then when I did speak it sounded very loud.

"It's not a bad night," I say. He didn't answer me. He said nothing until we came to a little village then he pointed to a little thatched house.

"How old is that little house?" he says.

"It's been there ever since I can remember," I say. He didn't say anything more for a while.

"I know Fergus," I say. He gave a little smile.

"Yes," he says. "I've seen you together."

"I like him," I say. He took a big deep breath.

"Fergus is a weak boy," he says. "He's a lazy boy."

"I didn't think he was all that lazy" I say.

"No," he says. "You wouldn't notice it in the village because they are all bloody lazy."

"There's not all that many jobs going around," I say.

"Over fifty per cent of the men in the village are out of work. If they wanted they could go and find work. Well, I'll bring the work to them and God help them if they don't do it."

I wasn't too sure what he meant.

"You mean you'll get them to sew things at home the way some of the women do?"

"I'll open up that half of the factory that has been closed down for years because of idleness," he says.

"I thought that part was in bad condition," I say.

"It just needs a few repairs," he says. Then he was silent. He tried to light his pipe while he was driving along, but it was hard and I think he was getting angry. I was going to offer to light it for him but I didn't get round to it.

He knew where I lived too, because he dropped me off at the corner. He was odd because I said good night to him and he didn't answer me. The men at the corner wouldn't be too pleased if they heard that he was going to open up the old half of the factory. But I had no need to tell them. They knew. I knew they knew when Jack Robinson says, "You'll not get me down there. I've got a blue card." That was because he lost an eye. If you lost an eye or anything like that you got a blue card and then it was harder for you to get a job.

"I got one too," Sam Kerr says. That was because he had

lost the fingers. Stewart was there as well and he thought it was funny because he wouldn't have to work because he didn't sign on and they couldn't send for him. But they had all been sent for jobs before and didn't get them. The thing is, if you're signing on and they send you to a job you have got to go or they cut your money off. But if you work it right when you go for the job, they write NOT SUITABLE on the card and you still get the money. They say that they sent Sam Kerr for this job and he had to keep threading this nylon or something through these little holes, and he kept making his hand jump so they said he was no good.

"You get more on the bloody dole than you would get down there," Jack Robinson says. "That man's getting too big for his boots. Somebody'll bring him down a bit."

"Well, that's what they said," Stewart says. "They said he was a go-ahead man."

"Go-ahead, my arse," Jack Robinson says. He was really angry.

"There's too many changes around here," Sam Kerr says.

"The smoke curls up from the factory chimney. They toil and sweat and live," the Poet says.

"You'll not be standing here reciting that stuff when he opens that place up," Jack Robinson says. Nobody usually paid much attention to the Poet and it was odd Jack Robinson saying that to him. But he paid no attention.

"The rivers run sweet over the gravel and stop when young maidens come. It runs, it runs. We all run and young maidens stop."

"I don't believe you ever had it," Rab says to the Poet. "I went with a virgin one night and took her maidenhead and I couldn't get her off me. She came around every night and tried to take my clothes off. She was lovely but she was too young."

I knew they would take it out on Fergus if he came down but

I couldn't do anything about it. He didn't know anything about what his Da was going to do, but still they took it out on him. He left his bicycle against the wall and came up to us.

"I was sorry to hear about Bill," he says to me.

"Oh, that's OK," I say.

"Move that bicycle," Jack Robinson says. Fergus looks at him and doesn't know whether to take him seriously or not. Then he looks at me.

"Maybe you'd better move it," I say. Fergus just stood there with his red waistcoat on. He looked a bit stunned.

"Are you going to move it?" Jack Robinson says. His neck was starting to get a bit red and the blue veins were coming out on it. He took a big sniff and you could see the veins wriggling under his skin like little snakes. He spat right on Fergus's shoe. "Can you hear all right?" he says.

"Let's be reasonable about this," Fergus says and he held out his little pink hands.

"What about your Da?" Sam Kerr says. "Is he reasonable?"

"Dad doesn't come into this," Fergus says. And he didn't know what to do with his little hands again. Jack Robinson went over and caught him by the shoulder and led him over to the bicycle.

"Do you see that?" he says. Fergus was getting a little bit shaky. You could hear it in his voice.

"Yes," he says. Everybody just stood and stared at him.

"Get it bloody moved," Jack says. Fergus kind of laughed.

"I really don't see why," he says. Jack shook him by the shoulder. Fergus took the bike by the handlebars.

"Well, all right, but I really don't see why." He wheeled it round to the back of the church.

"Maybe it's not his fault about his Da," I say. They all just sat there staring. They sat and stared at Fergus when he came back.

"Listen," Fergus says. "You are reasonable chaps. Can you tell me what I have done?"

Nobody spoke.

"We heard about your Da going to open up the other part of the factory," I say.

"Is he?" Fergus says. "Well, I should have thought you would all be pleased about that. It will bring more work to the village."

"Did anybody ever thump you one on the mouth?" Jack Robinson says. Sam Kerr gave an encouraging laugh.

"I am sorry if I have upset anyone," Fergus says.

"Right," Jack Robinson says and held out his hand to Fergus. Fergus put out his hand too.

"Friends," he says. But Jack Robinson caught his hand tight and squeezed it. Fergus let out a little yelp. Then Jack loosened his grip a bit.

"Let me try on that lovely waistcoat of yours," he says. Then he gave his hand another tight squeeze.

"Yes," Fergus says. "You can try it on." Jack let him go and Fergus took off his jacket and then the waistcoat.

"I don't want to do anybody any harm," Fergus says, and reaches the waistcoat to Jack. Jack put it on on top of his dirty overalls. It was too tight.

"It's lovely," he says, and he pulls off one of the brass buttons and throws it over the wall. Fergus didn't say anything. Jack held it together and walked up and down in front of everybody. They all said "Oh aye." Then Jack made a little skip like a woman and everybody clapped.

"I think I'll keep it," he says.

"Are you going to take Mary to the dance tomorrow night?" Stewart asks Fergus.

"Yes," Fergus says. "That is if you don't mind."

"The girl's in love with you," Stewart says. "What can I do about it?"

Fergus blushed.

"What are you blushing for?" Stewart says.

"I have got a tickle in my throat," Fergus says. Then he starts coughing.

"You better go home with a cough like that," Jack Robinson says.

"Perhaps you are right," Fergus says. "Can I have my waistcoat back please?"

"Bugger off," Jack says.

"Please," Fergus says. But it was no good, he wasn't going to get it back. He kept on asking for it but Jack seemed to be getting a bit annoyed with him again and in the end he left without it.

After he left Jack spent about ten minutes trying to throw the waistcoat up onto the telegraph wires. When it landed on them everybody cheered.

They all knew that Mary would do anything for Stewart and Stewart said that he would get her to go to the dance with Fergus the next night. He would think up something for a bit of a laugh. He knew the bloke that was doing MC at it too. He said that if Mary didn't follow his plan he would take her for a ride in the car up the mountain and then throw her out. They thought of all sorts of things. Somebody suggested that they would try and get him to take his clothes off then they would hide them. Jack Robinson suggested that they should try and get them into the toilet and then lock the door. He knew the toilets round at the back of the church hall, there was a bar on the outside. They argued about that for a while because Rab said that he had been in there with a girl and he locked it from the inside.

When Fergus called up the next day I told him that maybe he better not go to the dance. But he was serious about it. He said that he wouldn't let a girl down. He said that he had never let a girl down before. He had brought a big box of chocolates with him for me to take to Bill. I felt really sorry for him because the doctor had had the results from the X-ray and he was all clear, and he had bought a box of chocolates to give to Mary too. He wrote a note on the chocolates for Bill saying "Get well soon". But Bill was in no mood for the chocolates. They had given him some tablets and they made him really drowsy. He could hardly speak to me. His eyes kept closing and he would drift off to sleep. I tried to tell him about things but he couldn't take it in. Ma was well pleased when I told her. She said that they might be trying out a new drug that would cure him. When Da came home she had made up her mind that it was a new drug. She told him that it seemed to be working. Da didn't pay much attention because it was Friday night and he had got a big pay packet. Ma had taught him never to open his pay packet until he came home when they first got married and Da stuck to it. It was great because we were all excited because the packet was bigger than usual. Ma said that she thought it was a tax rebate but she was saying nothing. Da had got a tax rebate one time before and he never asked for it.

"Make a cup of tea first, Ma," I say.

Ma made the tea quicker than I had ever seen her do it before. Da held the big brown envelope and his hands were trembling. He was nearly laughing out loud too. It was well stuck down and he had to tear it open, but he was careful not to tear the pound notes. He brought out a few notes and then there was something hard still stuck inside. He tore it a little bit and brought out his cards with a little note inside it. He picked it up and read it. Then his face changed and I thought he was going to cry. It said that Da had been suspended until further notice for smoking while working with inflammable material.

Da didn't cry – but he did nearly. I think it was Ma going on that kept him back. She went on and on. I tried to tell her that it wasn't Da's fault but then she got onto me. She said that I was no good. None of us were any good. Da had just got the sack and I would never get a job and Bill was mad. Then she started crying and I thought I better get out.

I met Mary down the street but she didn't stop long. She was rushing home to get ready for the dance. But she wasn't getting ready because of Fergus – that was just going to be a joke before she went for a ride with Stewart in the car.

"Maybe you should just let Fergus be," I say.

"Don't be a spoilsport," she says. "It's just a bit of a laugh. Stewart's really looking forward to it. He brought me up a box of chocolates today."

"Fergus?" I say.

"God no," she says. "Stewart. If Fergus come up to our house with a box of chocolates I would tell him where to stick them."

"It's not right," I say.

"What do I care about the slimy little bugger?" she says. Then for the first time I realized how cruel she was. I looked at her. Her lips were tight. She even looked a bit ugly, like a witch or something. The whites of the eyes were like little bubbles of gravy and her skin seemed to be scaly.

I turned out of the village towards the country. Maybe she wasn't like that. Maybe that's just the way I seen her in my mind. I thought maybe I would never come back to the village. I would just keep on walking. Maybe I just want to cry and cry. Da sitting there and his mouth twitching and not knowing what to say and maybe him wondering what he could say to people when they asked him why he's not working. He might not be able to say anything in case he cries. Fergus getting ready. Poor Fergus with all that stuff he got from the chemist's and that box of chocolates too. And maybe him happy and maybe telling his Ma about Mary. And all that time Bill lying there in the hospital maybe thinking and thinking and not knowing. Maybe he's sad too. Maybe he misses me because he knows I love him. I love his poor big head. I feel as if my body is full of strings and they are all pulling in different directions. I see Jack Robinson tearing off that button on the little red waistcoat. Maybe I just want to cry. I can't stop it. I can feel the grass cutting against my face and my eyes are burning and my stomach gives big heaves. Oh God God God. My nose is all stuffed up and I breathe through my dry mouth and my cheeks are burning. I waken up and my cheeks are dry and sore and my head is sore too and it's nearly dark.

Fergus was standing up a bit from the corner when I got to the village. He was sparkling. They were all looking at him. He was wearing grey flannel trousers and a black blazer and a red and black tie. From where I was standing I could smell him. He smelt like a chemist's shop. Everybody was taking big long sniffs. He had the big box of chocolates with him too. They had big red roses painted on the lid. Every now and then he would look at his watch. It was half-past eight and Mary should have met him at eight o'clock. We all looked up the street to see if there was any sign of her, but there wasn't. Then everybody's mouth opened at the same time. It was Bill. He was marching down the street as if he owned the place. I went and met him.

"What are you doing out?" I say.

"What do you think? They thought I was mad but I let them know better. I signed myself out. I was better as soon as I stopped taking them tablets they gave me."

"Them was to cure you," I say.

"Cure my arse," he says. "All they did was make me sleep

all the time. You know that place was sending me mad. One bloke in there reckoned he was a king. I tried to tell him the truth but it made no difference. And another bloke. He thought he was in a bus and he was a conductor. He kept going on at people for not paying the fares. You know he hit one bloke."

"He signed himself out," I say to them at the corner. Everybody told him he done the wrong thing. They said he wouldn't get better doing that.

"You're all neurotic," Bill says. "You all need treatment. Look at you all standing there." He took a step back and looked at everybody. "Jasus," he says. "You want to take a look at yourselves." Then he started talking seriously.

"Look," he says. "I'm well in with one of the doctors up there. If you want I'll arrange for you all to see him. He might be able to do something. That's if it's not too late."

"You're not safe out," Rab says. "You should be locked up. You might rape some little girl or something."

"Who's to blame if you do something like that?" Jack Robinson says. "Is it the doctor or who?"

"You," Bill says. "If I kill somebody you'll get the rope."

"Don't talk nonsense," Jack Robinson says.

"I gave your name as a guardian," Bill says.

"I'm no bloody guardian," Jack says. Then he realized that Bill was just taking the piss out of him, and he went to hit him a slap on the ear but Bill came up quick and hit him on the wrist.

The woman that looked after the church hall came down to open it. They called her husband Mash because she fed him on mashed potatoes all the time. He had them for breakfast, tea and supper. She walked as if her knickers were wet all the time. In the winter time if there was snow on the ground she put chains round her wellington boots to keep from slipping.

Bill always had something to say to her. "Hallo, good-looking," he says. She tried not to look at him. Then he says when she was up level with him, "Take this in your hand and walk towards me." Her face got red but she waddled on.

Fergus seen Stewart coming in with Mary beside him but he looked away quick and pretended to be concentrating hard on something else. Stewart beeped the horn and stopped just down below him, but he didn't move. Then Stewart drove off again and blew the horn going past us. You could hear him blasting the horn all the way up the street and back down again. This time he drove up level with Fergus and Mary got out. Everybody clapped.

"Jasus, did you smell him?" Stewart says when he stopped with us. We were all watching Fergus. We saw him give Mary the chocolates and she gave them back to him. Then his face went really red and he tried to offer them to her again, but she still didn't take them. When they walked down past us everybody let out great loud whistles.

There was all sorts of people going to the dance from all over the countryside. They were walking, running, coming on motor-bikes, old cars, bikes – everything. Then when we knew there would be a good crowd there we decided to go up. We didn't go in straight away. We hung around outside the door. The little man at the door taking the money was hard to get past. Jack Robinson talked to him for a while. They talked about the weather and people they both knew and all the time he was easing himself in. Then when he got in he got up round to the back door and let us all in. The little man at the door couldn't remember who had paid and who hadn't by that time.

All the men were at one side of the hall and all the girls were at the other. The chap was playing the accordion and his son was playing the piano but nobody was dancing. That's the way it always was. It took a long time before it got going. It took two or three blokes to get up and go straight over and get the girls up, then more would get up. Fergus was standing near the door with the big box of chocolates and Mary was with the girls at the other side.

The MC got up and shouted, "Come on lads, come on. Where's your spirit? When I was your age you couldn't keep me off the floor." They say he was one for the girls when he was young, but he ended up marrying an old hag from the city. She was about the ugliest woman I had ever seen. It's odd, you would think if he had tried with his eyes closed he couldn't have anything worse. Still they say she had money. He was OK except for having no teeth. He got them all out one time and never got round to getting false ones in.

The girls sniggered when we all went down to Fergus. It was a slow foxtrot or something that was on and still there was nobody on the floor.

"Come on," Bill says to Fergus. "Let it go."

"I don't want to be first," Fergus says.

"Somebody's got to be first," Jack Robinson says. Then he got behind Fergus and tried to push him out onto the floor. He held back for a bit. But the floor was slippery and he started sliding. Jack pushed him right out then let him go and he fell on his backside. Everybody cheered and when Fergus got up he went straight to Mary. I reckon he did that because if he had come back to where we were standing Jack Robinson would have pushed him again. But Mary didn't want to dance with him. He asked the girl next to her but she didn't want to dance either. She was holding hands with another girl and they both giggled. Fergus turned round with a really red face and went to come back but Jack signs at him to go on and try another girl. He went and tried three or four girls but none of them would dance. Then he went to the ugliest girl in the room, Butch. She never missed a dance and she was always alone. She was more like a man than a woman. She wore boots and man's trousers and braces. She had big red eyes and wiry hair and stood with her hands in her pockets like a man too. Maybe it wasn't right to laugh at her because she was a bit simple. She was mad to get a man. No matter where you went to a dance she was always there. She was always first there too. Fergus put his arm round her big thick waist and led her onto the floor. She was wearing a sweater that was too short for her and too tight too and you could see her braces sticking out under it. Everybody was killing themselves laughing. Then Bill started to give a running commentary on them.

"Yes, they're on the floor," he says. "Butch is leading. A fine big girl. Trained by Bill Williams and rode several times by Bertie Orr. They move around the room now. Fergus is a young chap with not too much experience, but he is willing to go. They move up the hall now. What's this? What's this? Fergus swings her round – has Butch lost her balance? No, she's still going. The tension is growing here tonight. Butch is weighing fourteen stone, but she has been in steady training. Fergus has been all over the world and it has been said that he has challenged bigger girls. But has he the weight? Butch is looking into his eyes. This girl is a tiger. But Fergus remains calm. Now he swings her again but she stays on her feet. It will take more than that to get this tiger down. Look at his movement. Now Fergus lets himself go on the corner. The crowd cheer but he is still smiling."

The music stops and Fergus leads her back to the other girls. The box of chocolates are on the floor where he left them when he asks her to dance. He picks them up and she takes them. Then he has to walk all the way back to where we were. We all clapped and patted him on the back. But he had helped to get it going because in the next dance there were several people up. When it really got warmed up, Jack Robinson and Sam Kerr went and danced together. Stewart was angry because Mary didn't want to dance with Fergus. He wanted her to do some dance with him that would make him take his clothes off. He had it arranged with the bloke who was playing the music to look out for Fergus crossing the white line. We had played that game before. You see, there was a white square painted on the floor and the idea was that if you were just across or on this square when the music stopped the boy had to take off an item of clothing. But Fergus didn't know anything about it and asked Mary, but she wouldn't do it and he had to do it with Butch again. Fergus marched round the floor with her several times with a big grin and not knowing what was going to happen to him. A few people had taken their ties off and Fergus was OK. But then it started to happen to him. He thought it was a great joke the first time when he just had to take off his tie. But then it happened every time to him. He had his shoes and socks off and his tie and shirt and still the music went on and stopped every time he went over the white line. When it came to him having to take his trousers off he wouldn't do it, but everybody started booing and he took them off. He was wearing bright red underpants. Everybody cheered and he was pleased. Then the next thing he had to do was to take them off. But he wouldn't – he tried to run. Butch got hold of him and everybody was cheering. She was trying to pull them down and he was trying to pull them up. In the end he got away and into the cloakroom, but she was after him and the next thing was he came out of there and up the floor holding his clothes tight. There was a little thing like a bite out of one of the legs of his pants too. Everybody was hysterical. She was after him. He got in first to the little room at the back and he must have been able to bolt the door because she tried it and couldn't get it open. That was the end of Fergus that night. After he went in there he must have put on his clothes and got out the back door. After that everybody was laughing all the time. And everybody was dancing too. Big Butch stood there but nobody asked her to dance after that and I seen her starting off to walk home on her own when it was over.

Stewart was really angry with Mary for not having Fergus on. She said she couldn't with everybody looking at her. Stewart asked her if she was scared of people or what. Then she started crying and Stewart paid no attention to her. He just stood and talked to us as if she wasn't there. But she still stood there. She wanted him to take her home. You could tell that. In the end I reckon she was getting on his nerves because he told her to jump in. She stopped crying then. He told Bill and me that he would take us home too. She sat in the front seat – not crying, but she gave a little sniff now and then.

"What's up?" Stewart says.

"Nothing," she says and blew her nose on a little bit of toilet paper she had tucked up her sleeve.

"You could do worse than get Fergus," Stewart says.

"Stop pulling my leg," Mary says.

"No, I'm serious," Stewart says.

"You know who I want," she says.

"I don't," Stewart says. "Tell me."

"You know," she says. Stewart looks round at Bill and me.

"Do you two know?" he says.

"It's me," Bill says.

"Is it Bill?" Stewart says.

"Don't be silly," Mary says and she hit him a little pat on the leg.

"Who is it then?" he says.

"I'm not going to tell you," she says. Stewart slows the car down.

"Well, if you're not going to tell me you might as well get out," he says, and he opens her side before the car had stopped.

She caught him by the sleeve and kind of cried, "It's you."

Stewart laughs. "Me," he says. "What would you do with a boy like me? I'm no good." Then he looks round at us. "Am I?" he says.

"No, you're not," Bill says.

"There you are," Stewart says. He pulls the door closed and moves away.

"You would be better with somebody like Fergus," he says. "Look at me. I'm not very good-looking or anything."

"I think you are," Mary says.

"What makes you think that?" he says.

"Don't get me going Stewart," she says.

"I'm serious," he says. "I'm no good. You would be better with somebody like Fergus. He's reliable. Not like me. You can never tell when I'm going to turn up and for all you know I might have a girl somewhere else."

"No Stewart," she says. She was nearly crying again. I reckon he was wanting her to cry.

"You can't trust me," he says. "For all you know I could be anywhere with another girl." He took a little brooch out of his pocket and looks at it. Then he threw it into the front pocket of the car. "God knows where I got that from," he says. But Mary says nothing. He looks at her kind of sideways and then at the road again. "I might as well tell you," he says. "I gave a girl a lift home last night from a dance."

"Is that all you did?" Mary says.

"Well, I can't tell you everything," Stewart says.

"Maybe I would be wise to go out with a nice boy like Fergus," she says.

"That's what I like to hear," Stewart says. "There's big

money in that family. You go out with him. You would be better. I don't want to get tied down with one girl."

"I didn't mean that," Mary says.

"You must have meant it or you wouldn't have said it," Stewart says. "I don't want to go out with a girl that has her eye on somebody else."

"I didn't mean it," she says.

"Ah, come on," Stewart says. "You mean it all right."

"I didn't honestly," she says. Stewart pulls up outside her house.

"Get out," he says and sits and looks at her.

Then she starts sobbing. "Believe me, Stewart," she sobs.

"If you meant what you say you would let me," he says. "Maybe they're right. You are a little prick teaser." She kind of stops crying and feels up her arm for the little bit of toilet paper.

"Get out," Stewart shouts. Then she is worse than ever. She opens the door and gets out, but she doesn't go too far away from the car. Stewart moves forward slightly and stops. She comes up to the window and looks in. Stewart just sat and looked at her for a minute. Then he turns the window down.

"Stewart," she says.

"What do you want?" he says.

"I would let you," she says. He leans over and opens the door.

"Get in," he says. "And if you're having me on you better take what you get."

When she got in Stewart didn't lose any time in getting us home. "Don't do anything I wouldn't do," Bill shouts at him when we got out.

"That's leaving me plenty of scope," Stewart shouts and drove off. We could hear the car long in the night air. You could hear him changing gear really plain. They were going up towards the bog road.

Ma had forgotten to leave the key below the mat and Bill and me had to climb in the back window. But we might as well have wakened them up in the first place because as soon as we switched on the light Ma and Da were downstairs. Ma was pushing Da in front of her and Da was holding back a bit. He was in his shirt-tails and he was protecting his balls with both hands.

"I said it was nobody," he says. Ma gave him a push right into the kitchen.

"They could take the whole house for all you care," she says. Da got both hands round his balls again and ran up the stairs.

"You get no bloody peace in this house," he says. Ma sat down on the sofa as if she was about to pass out or something. Then she screwed up her face.

"You better go to bed too," Bill says.

"I can't sleep," Ma shouts. "What the hell do you care?"

"No need to eat me," Bill says.

"If you had a stomach like mine you couldn't sleep either. And your Da doesn't care. All he wants to do is lie up there in his stinking bed. What does he care?" Then she let a loud shout upstairs. But Da didn't answer. She sat for a minute with a pained expression on her face then she let out another shout.

"Come up to bed and give me peace," he shouts. Ma sat there with the pained expression on her face. Every now and then it got worse, as if she had the toothache or something.

"Get up to bed and don't get on my nerves," Bill says.

"Shut your mouth," Ma snarls.

"I'll not shut it for you," Bill says.

"You don't care," Ma says. "You wouldn't care if I was dying – you would just sit there."

"I reckon it's all in the mind," Bill says. Ma let out another loud scream up the stairs to Da. Then you could hear Da getting out of bed. He came right down and got hold of Ma.

"Come up to bloody bed," he says.

"If you wouldn't stand with your arse to the fire all the time you wouldn't get them piles," Bill says. Ma pushes Da away and his shirt slipped off his shoulders.

"I reckon you're cracking up," Bill says. Then Ma got a big pain and she hits out at Da.

"All you want is the one thing," she says.

"What can I do?" Da says, and he stands there kind of helpless looking.

"You could get cold water," Ma says. Da shakes his head as much as to say he can take no more, then he goes in and gets a basin of cold water.

"I'm not going to watch this," Bill says. "It's enough to give you nightmares."

Bill and I went up to bed but we kept our doors open when there was going to be a row. We didn't want to hear but we had to listen all the same.

"Go easy, go easy," Ma shouts.

"My God, I'm doing my best," Da says. "You should get them seen to."

"You're all the bloody same," Ma says. "You wanted me when I didn't have them."

"What can I do?" Da says. "Does that make them any easier?" Then Ma let out a loud scream.

"You tried to hurt me," she shouts. "I'll try it myself." Then there was silence for a while.

"Come up to bed and don't keep everybody awake," Bill shouts. Then you could hear them shouting at each other and things flying. You couldn't hear what they were saying, but the language was bad all right and half crying. Then Da came upstairs and into my room. His shirt was soaking wet and he was nearly crying.

"I try my best," he says then goes into his own room. Ma

stayed downstairs for a while and I thought maybe Da had hit her with something. But he hadn't. Later she came up and got into my bed. I didn't like the feel of her beside me. It's odd, I didn't want to touch her. Every now and then she gave a little moan. But I got it out of my mind and in the end we all went asleep with the landing light still on.

Nobody mentioned it in the morning and Ma and Da didn't speak to each other. I thought the best thing to do was to get out till the air cleared. Bill came with me. Bill didn't want to go to see Fergus to see if he was all right after the dance but I said I was going anyway so he came.

It was his Da and the two big dogs that opened the door.

"Is Fergus in?" I say.

"No," he says, and Bill and me just stood there. We didn't know whether to walk away or just stay.

"Will he be out for long?" I ask.

"He has gone to the city with his Mum to buy some books. He will be going to university soon you know, so he has a bit of reading to do."

"I read a lot of books when I was in the bin," Bill says. Then we all stood there and didn't look at each other. Or maybe he was looking at us.

"Maybe you better come in," he says. You could tell he didn't mean it but still we went in.

"It must be worth some money, this place," Bill says and he walks round the room and took a close look at everything. Fergus's Dad went into a little cupboard and brought a bottle of lemonade and gave Bill and me a glass each. He had a big glass of whisky for himself.

"Shouldn't you be down in the factory?" Bill says, and sank down into one of the big chairs.

"No," Fergus's Dad says. "I am just staying here to have a look at the new plans."

"So you're going to open up that bit of the factory?" Bill says.

"Yes," Fergus's Dad says. "We will be moving in the new machinery any day now." Then he looked very thoughtful and he didn't speak for a bit. He poured out another big glass of whisky for himself. "I only wish Fergus would come in with me. I own most of the shares now and if he came in and took an interest he could be a great help." It must have been the drink that was making him talk or something because nobody in the village had ever had a conversation with him before.

"Fergus is smart," I say. He looks at me as if he didn't know what I was on about.

"He means if he reads too many books he'll crack up," Bill says. Then Fergus's Dad picks up one of the papers that were lying on the floor.

"Can you understand this stuff?" he says. He looks at Bill very seriously. "I got to where I am now by myself. I had very little schooling but I educated myself. I worked hard. It didn't come easy."

"Do you reckon it's worth it?" Bill says. He looks at Bill as much as to say are you mad. Then he seemed to get a bit angry.

"I'm going to make this village work. I'm going to change things around here. What has anybody ever done around here to earn their keep? I will let them see that you can't always scrounge from society."

"I don't reckon nobody wants to work," Bill says.

"It's not what they want, it's what they are going to get." He poured out another big whisky.

"Da got the sack from the factory," I say. "He was smoking."

"I have materials worth thousands of pounds down there. I can't afford to take risks. But he will be sent for when I need him. Now if you two boys can leave me now, I have work to get on with." I got up but Bill sat until he had finished his lemonade.

Fergus's Dad was right. In two or three days all sorts of big machines came into the factory and men to fix them too. Nobody was pleased. They all stood at the corner and shook their heads. All but the Poet that is. He had taken to standing outside the butcher's. He stood there every day. Sometimes he would stand and watch the butcher carve up the meat and sometimes he would just stand with his arms folded and look up and down the street. Bill reckoned that he was cracking up. A lot of the men at the corner thought that it was odd too. But they said nothing.

Things had changed at the corner. Stewart didn't stop too much now and if he did and somebody said something to him about Mary, he told them to mind their own business. But still she was seen with him in the car a few times. Then he just started to drive past her and the next thing we heard was that she was pregnant. Maybe that was even before she knew herself. Fergus still came to the corner with me and Bill, but nearly every night they did something to him. One night Jack Robinson twisted his arm so badly that he passed out. But he was good about it. I told him that he only did it in fun and he believed me. They were always scheming up things to do to him. They even got a pair of scissors and gave him a stupid haircut because they told him that Mary would like him better. Even after all that he liked them. He said they were honest natural folk. Anyway it was Mary that got them to cut his hair just for the laugh. They got her to write him silly love letters too asking him to meet here somewhere, then she wouldn't turn up or if she did turn up she would have him on.

It got around to everybody knowing that she was going to

have a baby and she asked him if he would marry her even if the baby wasn't his. He said he would. But Bill reckoned she was cracking up too, because she started going out with all sorts of blokes. And she tried to stand in front of Stewart's car to get him to stop. But he never did, and the next thing we knew he had gone to England. Fergus told me that he thought he really was in love with her. He said that she wouldn't write him them letters unless she really meant it. He didn't know that most of them had been made up by the blokes at the corner. He believed the letters even when Mary was really nasty to him. She had got nasty to every man. She just went out with them to get what she could for nothing. One night Fergus came up to me and told me all about what he did to her. You couldn't tell whether he had gone the whole way or not. But there's one thing he didn't tell me to the end. She had made him pay five pounds. That was the night he left his bicycle in at the back of the church to go for a walk with her and when he came back somebody had sliced his tyres with a knife. The main reason they did that was because his Dad had put a thing in the paper to say that the other part of the factory would be opening soon. Fergus didn't care about the tyres. He said that he had experienced something that he would never forget. He was due to go to Oxford the next week and he couldn't make up his mind. He thought maybe he might marry Mary. I couldn't tell him that she would never marry anybody only Stewart and he was in England. His Dad wanted him to stay and come into the factory with him but his Mum wanted him to go and in the end he did. It was odd the night before he went. He cried and he even had to give me a real kiss too. The next day he wasn't there any more.

In a funny sort of way I missed him because Bill had taken to his bed again. I told him that Fergus would write to me and everything but he didn't even answer. Da had got his job back again but he didn't care about that either. One day he cried all day and I had to go for the doctor. He wouldn't go into hospital either and the doctor couldn't make him, but he gave him the same pills that he had last time he was in. He had to take them three times a day and two at night. Ma was sure they would make him better. I gave him two and a glass of water before I went to bed and I thought maybe he would be better in the morning too. I prayed to God to make me ill instead of him. I prayed that the pills would work that night. But they didn't. I went in in the morning and his big head was hanging half out of bed and there was a little bit of vomit hanging out of his mouth. The empty pill bottle was lying on the floor and he was dead. Ma wouldn't believe it. She said it was the way the pills worked. They knocked you out for a while. It's odd because when the doctor told her she said maybe it was better that way. My mind couldn't think for a few days. It was as if there was nothing in my head but air.

There was only Da and me and two uncles that I had never seen before to carry the coffin to the graveyard.

The Friday after the funeral an extra man came to pay out the dole. He took us all to the side and gave us cards to take to the factory and if we didn't start we would get no more money. We would be OK if they wrote NOT SUITABLE on the cards but they didn't. We all had to start on the Monday. I got a letter from Fergus that day. He said that he missed us all very much and he missed his Mum and Dad and most of all he missed Mary.

Everybody had a chance to see the letter before his Dad came round the place and everybody had to get stuck into work. There was all sorts of machines there. The one I was working was easy. The cloth rolled off one roller and into some kind of stuff and onto another roller. Then when it was all on the other roller, I pulled a handle and it stopped and somebody came along and took it away to be dried or something. There was a lot of chemicals to mix into the water that the cloth went through.

Jack Robinson and Sam Kerr had to put cloth into these big vats and then turn water into them and boil it in bleach after they put the big iron lid down. Nobody liked their job and nobody liked old Moore. He did everything but kick us. If you lifted your eyes off whatever you were doing for a second he was sure to be standing behind you. "Get your bloody finger out," he would shout.

Jack Robinson worked at slow motion even when old Moore was standing behind him. You could see old Moore's neck getting redder and redder and Jack would be boiling up inside like the big vats of bleach. It was as if they both wanted to scratch the skin off each other. You felt that you couldn't walk between them because there would be something bad there. Strung from neck to neck. Old Moore seemed to be everywhere. He seemed to be behind several people at the same time. The Poet was the only one that didn't go to the factory. When they gave him the card he just said, "It's beautiful. Thin as a razor and slices into the heart of the pure."

Jack Robinson didn't know what to do to get back at old Moore. One day a group of them got together at lunchtime and worded a letter to Fergus. They pretended it had come from Mary. It said that she really loved him and would he come back and marry her. She seen it and thought it was great and she added a lot of romantic things to it. Everybody thought it was great. They said that Fergus would come back and they could tell him to get stuffed. They wrote one to Fergus's Dad too telling him that his son had put an innocent girl up the shoot and what was he going to do about it. And at the end they said, "If you take my advice you'll go and get fucked."

I wasn't going to give them the address to write to Fergus but when I took the letter out of my pocket somebody had already torn the address off it. Then Mary told them not to worry because if Fergus came back she would already be in England. She had had a letter from Stewart and he had asked her to come over.

The Poet was standing outside the butcher's when they went to post the letter but when they came back he wasn't there. There was a little group of people standing outside. The butcher had nipped through to the back yard for something and as soon as he went the Poet just nipped in and sliced his throat open.

That was at lunch-time and nobody went back to work that day. Old Moore was mad. He told everybody that they would lose a day's pay. Jack Robinson said that if he lost a day's pay there would be trouble and so did Sam Kerr and everybody else. But when pay day came there was more than a day's pay missing from everyone's packet. Old Moore stood behind Jack Robinson and Sam Kerr for the rest of the afternoon because they were working extra slow. The cloth went into the vat all right and the bleach and then the boiling water. But nobody knew till the vat had been boiling for several hours and the big iron lid was lifted that old Moore was in there too. Earlier on in the week old Moore had said to me, "Keep the good work up son." Maybe I liked him for that.

But that wasn't the end. When we all moved out of the factory we all stood and looked. Then we seen the smoke starting to rise from the singeing room and the flames started crackling right through the building. Everybody just stood. It was as if they all knew it was going to happen.

I had a very jolly letter from Fergus the next morning. It said that he had this great letter from Mary and he was going to give up university and come back and marry her and help his Dad in the factory. He said he felt great and his Dad would be pleased when he wrote to tell him. But he said he just had to tell me first because he knew I would be happy about him and Mary.

Dear Fergus,

Don't come,

Johnny.

LITTLE SISTER

Margaret Gaan

When Little Sister comes from Wahu to visit her grandparents in Shanghai she is drawn into the passionate conflicts stirring China towards revolution. Head of the household is Grandmother, who with her bound Lily Feet belongs to the traditions of an old China now vanishing. Yet her compassion and understanding hold the family together through their loves, their griefs, their bewilderments.

Bemused by the social changes in Shanghai, Little Sister is also witness to the growing secret love between her cousin Celia and their adopted cousin 'Lik'. A love that brings them confusion as well as happiness: Lik is torn between his love for Celia and his dedication to the revolution, but it is his hidden past that dictates the course for them both . . .

'a touching, compassionate novel' *Literary Review*

'poignant picture of a vanished society . . . memorable' *Irish Times*

Futura Publications
Fiction
0 7088 2538 9

SUMMER AT THE HAVEN

Katharine Moore

'Warmhearted without being sentimental . . . an unusual achievement' Robert Nye, *The Guardian*

Mrs Thornton lives in the attic because she prefers it. Surrounded by intimate memorials of her past, she counts her blessings:

. . . she is not deaf, like old Miss Brown
. . . nor going blind, like Miss Norton
. . . nor arthritic like Miss Dawson
. . . nor bald, like Miss Ford
. . . nor bronchial like Mrs Perry
. . . nor (thank God) wandering in her mind, like Mrs Langley

For Mrs Thornton is one of the eight residents of The Haven, a private home for elderly ladies, which, like its occupants, has seen better times.

Shrewd, warm-hearted, funny, unsentimental, SUMMER AT THE HAVEN is that rarest of novels: a book about old age that shines with optimism.

Futura Publications
Fiction
0 7088 2516 8